Dynamic Image Publications Presents

The Last Bachelor Left

By Christian Cashelle

Dynamic Image Publications Presents
The Last Bachelor Left
By Christian Cashelle
ISBN: 979-8-9852060-1-2

Edited by: Jasmine Clayborn

Manufactured in the United States of America

Other titles by Christian Cashelle

The Harris Series:
Move the Needle

The Ava Trilogy:
Ava's Story
When All Else Fails
My Mother's Child

The Camryn Series:
My Joy
Gino's Revenge

Revisions of Life
Birds in the Rain

To you,

Learn to choose yourself and stick to your standards. Don't let anyone overstep your boundaries… even if it is the last bachelor left.

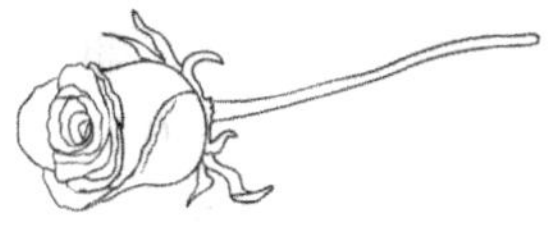

One | The Bachelor

"You are the biggest jerk I've ever met. It surprises me that you even get ass."

Julian Harris laughed before taking a sip of his Hennessey on the rocks. He licked his lips as the burn filled his chest, looking over at the beauty who stood with a frown on her face. Carmen was fine, there was no doubt about that. Julian noticed her beauty the first time Sage introduced them. She was slimmer than his usual type, but her beautiful, brown skin and flawless face made up for it. There were two things about her that he didn't like; her height and her attitude.

"Thank you, sweetheart. You aren't always a ray of sunshine when I see you either." Julian wished she wasn't as tall as him so he could look down at her. She rolled her eyes and gave him a fake smile.

Julian wasn't usually so quick to banter with women, but something about Carmen always made him go there. Most of the time it was playful, but he could tell when it got serious for her and that always irritated him. A woman who could dish quirky remarks out, but not take them was a pet peeve of his. Of course, every time he saw her he would take it there.

He looked around the half-empty lounge trying to think of something to say, knowing that her comeback was on the tip of her tongue. The cocktail tables that filled the room were covered in black linen tablecloths that matched those of the booths around the walls. Each one had a small votive candle in the middle. That seemed to be the only decor in the room. Julian figured since most of the businesses downtown had been closed the past few months due to covid, decoration really wasn't a main priority. Julian had to admit that his priorities were shifting when it came to life in general as well. Living through a pandemic made a lot of things less of a priority these days.

"Will you two cut it out," Sage said. "I thought you two were friends." Julian thought friend was a bit of a stretch when it came to Carmen. She was his cousin's woman's best friend. That was too many titles to even give her that energy. The smirk on her face let Julian know that they were on the same page.

"We just had a common goal to put you two out of your misery," Carmen said, waving her finger between Sage and Pierre. "We did that, now there's no need for pleasantries."

Sage shook her head and parted her lips to say something else. Julian watched his cousin wrap his arm around Sage's waist and whisper in her ear. No doubt telling her anything to get her to lay off her match-making attempt. Julian was content when he realized his cousin's charm worked.

He had only stepped out that night with the couple because he was overworked and stir crazy. Now that a lot of the restrictions with Covid were lifting and he was fully vaccinated, Julian was ready to be outside. However, his wingman had been happily in a relationship for the last 6 months. It was putting a damper on his escapades.

Last year, when he hired Sage as a business consultant, he never thought she would become part of their lives. You would be surprised at how in love Sage and Pierre were with the way they were at each other's throats. After a while, Julian could tell that Pierre really liked her, which is why he teamed up with Carmen in the first place. The couple was too stubborn for their own good and needed someone to knock some sense into them. Julian could admit that Carmen was fine, but that attitude was not.

"You don't have any other friends?" Julian asked Sage, deciding he wasn't done bothering Carmen for the night.

"Nope," Sage said, popping the 'p'. "Just my sister."

"Just your sister, huh?" Pierre said. Sage blushed before running her index finger over his jawline.

"Aw baby, you're my favorite friend," she said before leaning in to kiss him. Julian gave them a dead stare while Carmen pushed back from the table, stepping backward with her arms stretched out and her fingers on the edge of it.

"I'm going to get some alcohol," she said. Julian nodded before getting up to follow her.

"Was this supposed to be a double date?" he asked, leaning over to get closer to her ear. Carmen looked at him and frowned.

"I didn't know you or Pierre were coming," she admitted. "I can really go home."

"Let me give you a ride," Julian said, quickly. Carmen frowned but Julian held his hands up in surrender. "Not like that. I just ain't trying to be out with them either."

Carmen leaned against the bar closer to the clear divider, drawing the attention of the lady bartender a few feet away. "Two shots of Crown, please? …So what's our excuse to go?"

"Work?"

Carmen shook her head while running her fingers through the ends of her curls. "She knows I'm off tomorrow."

"Family emergency?"

"Too much."

"Hell, just say you got a headache or something," Julian said. "Women love that excuse."

Carmen side eyed him before taking her shot and laughing. "I shouldn't even give you this."

Julian smirked, taking the other shot from her. They clinked each other's glasses before taking them heads up. "Thank you, but you aren't buying me a shot."

Carmen slammed a $20 on the bar and put her glass on top of it. "Already paid for. Let's go."

After saying goodbye to Pierre and Sage, the two headed out and began walking down Washington Ave. Carmen pulled a small bottle of hand sanitizer out of her clutch, flipped the cap, and held it up to Julian. He smirked before holding his left hand out.

"Thank you."

"No worries."

He watched her long, decorated nails as she rubbed the liquid over them and then waved her hands out in the air. "I'm right here."

"Nice," Carmen said, stepping back to let him open the passenger door of his black F150. He smirked.

"This isn't a date."

"But you're still going to open my door," she snapped back. "Thank you."

Julian laughed before pulling the door open. He didn't wait until she was in before heading over to his side. When he got in, Carmen was laughing.

"You just can't help yourself can you?" she asked. Julian smiled and shook his head.

"Put your address in."

They drove without speaking for a few miles, letting Julian's random playlist fill the silence. Carmen sighed.

"So what's your deal?" she asked.

"My deal about what, love?" he asked, licking his lips.

"That!" she said, pointing at him as she turned in her seat. Julian frowned. "You got an off switch to flirting?"

Julian chuckled. "It wasn't a big deal. I just talk nice to the ladies. Don't read too much into it. Unless you want me to cuss you out or something."

"One extreme or the other huh?"

Julian frowned. "My flirting with you is extreme? I can stop."

Carmen laughed. "I'm just saying you know since you're fine women will take that flirting to heart. It's not like you one of these 'where my hug' men or something."

Julian chuckled but licked his lips. "You think I'm fine?"

Carmen side eyed him but the attraction was evident. Julian's almond complexion was void of any blemishes or marks outside of the small cut on his eyebrow. It didn't even look like a cut, almost just like a little patch of hair on his eyebrow didn't grow in fully. His slanted eyes were almost the same color as his skin which gave him an advantage whenever he looked at you. Carmen had never seen him without a clean haircut or his waves out of place. He had a smaller build than she preferred but since she wasn't mentally attracted to him, that didn't matter.

"You aight," she said after some moments of silence. Julian laughed.

"You don't have to lie, sweetheart," he said, confidently. "It's all in your face."

"So you're saying you aren't attracted to me?"

Julian eyed her while getting on Hwy 70. "Now what's your deal? Why would it matter if I was attracted to you? You can't stand me right?"

Carmen rolled her eyes "I'll take that as a yes."

Julian laughed. "We're both too grown to be doing this. We're attracted to each other but can't stand each other. We honestly are too much alike if you ask me."

Carmen looked at him for a second before nodding. "Friends it is."

"Bet, friend...put me on one of your homies."

Carmen laughed before swatting his shoulder. Julian didn't mind the resolve to remain platonic with Carmen. Outside of her physical appearance, Julian didn't feel any connection. He also knew he wasn't ready to settle down, and dealing with his cousin's woman's best friend would definitely end up awkward for all parties involved. He thought about taking a crack at Sage's sister, but decided she was off limits as well. Never mind the fact that he knew she was in a relationship. He didn't want to hear Pierre's mouth about it at all.

It took him about 20 minutes to pull up at Carmen's front door. She thanked him for the ride before jumping out of his truck. Julian went through his contacts to see who he would be spending the night with while he waited for Carmen to go inside. He might have been a jerk, but he was a gentleman.

Two | Trauma Untreated

The construction side of Harris Trucking & Construction had definitely taken a hit since the shutdown. Julian was grateful that he forced Pierre to hire Sage last year. With her help in finding ways for them to decrease costs, their profit margin was doing well before the pandemic. That had given them enough to pay a few employees and shareholders, holding them over. When the PPP loan for small businesses emerged, Pierre jumped on it. Julian was hesitant, but when the check hit- all was well. Pierre was working on ways to get the debt forgiven, but Julian was happy restrictions were lifting and construction contracts were coming back in. Income was a necessity if they would have to pay the loan back. Fortunately, construction season wasn't year round pre-pandemic anyway. So having a few months off wasn't abnormal. Granted, the shutdown was a little longer than just an off-season.

The office building where they rented a floor had only closed down for a few months due to the limited capacity they already worked in. The building assistant, however, had lost her position and everything was automated as far as entry and rent. Other than a few more cleaning measures, office life hadn't changed much.

Even though it was only a few months, Julian was glad to be back in his office. It was a change of pace from construction sites when Pierre pitched the idea about dispatching others to do jobs. Julian wasn't sold on the idea of sitting up in an office, but it grew on him. Not being there due to Covid made him miss it even more.

Trying to decide his course of action for the day, he decided to call his cousin from across the hall.

"Why are you bothering me?" Pierre said. "Didn't you just come in?"

"Mind the business that pays you, bro," he said. Pierre chuckled. "What you got on the schedule for the day?"

"Truck repairs," Pierre said.

"Ouch...anything I can do?"

"You bored over there?" Pierre asked. "Don't answer that...Sage calling me. I'll be over there in a minute."

Julian huffed as Pierre hung up on him. Instead of calling him back just to be worrisome, Julian turned on the mounted television on the adjacent wall and surfed through the guide until he got to a local news station. He wasn't a fan, but it helped him scout new business. Any developments or structures that were discussed led him down a wormhole of cold calling or reaching out to his network to get bid information.

His desk phone rang and he picked up quickly. "Harris Trucking and Construction."

"Hi, nephew!"

Julian smiled to hear the familiar voice on the line. "What's up, Aunt Janet? What do I owe the pleasure?"

She laughed. "You always talking slick, boy," she teased. "I was calling to fish for ideas to get your mom and dad for their anniversary."

Julian frowned before looking at the date on his desk calendar. "Auntie, you're shopping early aren't you?"

"Listen, that's all I've been doing since the shutdown." They both laughed. "And next month will be here before you know it. Now answer my question."

"I'm sending them to that spa they like so much in Chicago. That's all I could do after paying for this party."

"Deniece didn't help you? That girl…"

Julian didn't even respond. His sister didn't even have input on the party let alone add $5 to the cost. She'd show up as if she did though. Julian was sure of it.

"Momma's been talking about redoing the kitchen, maybe you can get something custom with the new design."

"She has been sending me Pinterest ideas."

Julian chuckled, knowing how they'd gotten hooked on the app a few years back.

Janet was Pierre's mom. Their dads; Jaren and Ray, were brothers. They were your typical bickering, loving siblings and their respective spouses had fallen into that dynamic after decades together. Julian always felt he could relate a little more to Uncle Jay than his own father though. Where Uncle Jay had been business savvy and willing to take risks, Ray Harris was the opposite. He worked the same job in welding before retiring to his pension. Safe and reliable is what he would say, Julian would call it predictable and boring.

Joyce and Ray Harris would be celebrating their 40th anniversary that following month. They'd married right out of high school, neither had plans for college. Back then if you got in at a factory, you stayed there. Ray Harris had done that and saved up enough money to buy his bride a nice home. Joyce was an elementary school teacher up until she had Deniece. Julian was 4 at the time. Joyce's heart was set on going back to work, but she couldn't leave her children in the hands of 'just ol' anybody' so Ray told her she could stay home. That was one thing he did admire most about his father. Ray loved Joyce out loud. Julian and Deniece had been witness to that their whole lives. Growing up, he didn't always appreciate their public displays of affection, but when he was old enough to know what love really was, his parents mirrored it.

"My son must know I'm on the phone with you," Aunt Janet said. "Love you. Talk to you later."

Julian chuckled. “Love you, too, Auntie.”

The short call with his aunt put his mind on the party at hand. He decided to check his emails to make sure everything was still in order and see who had sent in an RSVP so far. He was aware of Covid causing some to decline and that was fine by him. Julian wasn’t trying to feed all of St. Louis anyway.

He thought about what he would make Deniece do at the party since she hadn’t helped with anything else. The building manager offered a staff member for covid protocols and Deniece wouldn’t be helpful with that anyway. She’d just let everyone in without checking temperatures or anything.

Deniece was responsible when it came to her own business, but anything that didn’t immediately concern her was a waste of her time. Everyone in her life spoiled her, including Julian, so it wasn’t really her fault. However, Julian felt it was time for her to act her age. He couldn’t worry too much about it, so he took on the responsibility of planning their parents' party on his own. They deserved it, so it got done.

***

A few hours later, Julian was ready for lunch. It was amusing how he was so ready to be back in the office and now all he wanted to do was go home and relax. Julian sighed as Nicole’s bright, smiling face rounded the open door of his office.

“Hey,” she sang, waving before dropping a folder on his desk. “This was sent over from city hall.”

Julian nodded before taking the folder, dropping it in front of him on his desk, and sitting back in his chair. “Thanks.”

Nicole frowned. “You okay?”

“Just got a lot to do.”

She nodded before walking back towards the door. “I see. Well, we’ll talk later.”

"About what?" he asked. Nicole stopped walking. She looked over his face before biting the corner of her lip.

"Nothing in particular...I just meant...we haven't really talked since last weekend..outside of work stuff."

Julian's face softened. He hadn't really thought much about their last date and now he realized why Nicole was on edge with him all day.

"Right," he said. "Yeah, let's catch up. You got dinner plans?" he asked, finally looking up at her. She smiled.

"I can pencil you in."

Julian chuckled. "Do that."

Nicole was the office manager for Harris Trucking and Construction. She'd been promoted from assistant right before the pandemic. She and Julian had been on a few dates the last few months. Since they were around each other for work and texted regularly, Julian thought Nicole was the safest option to occupy his time during the pandemic. Julian could tell that Nicole wanted more, but he just wasn't all the way into it. She was cool to hang around and definitely looked good on his arm, but he wasn't looking for anything serious. She seemed to understand, but Julian could feel her getting attached. He thought about Pierre's hesitation for him to start dating her and knew it wouldn't end well.

Thoughts of his dating life escaped him as his cousin walked in, snatching his mask off in the process.

"What's wrong?"

"Tired of doing repairs. I told you I was going to the shop today for Jake's truck from that accident he had. Now one of the other trucks needs new tires."

"Nothing major."

"Still annoying," Pierre said. They both laughed as he sat down on the other side of his desk. Julian smirked. Pierre had been more relaxed since being with Sage.

"You staying late?"

"Nah, Baby got something planned at the crib," he said. Julian smirked. Prime example.

"You love that girl, don't you?" Julian teased his cousin. When he noticed the acknowledgment on Pierre's face, he stopped laughing. "P? For real."

"Yeah, man. I do," Pierre said, running his hand down his face before smiling. "I love the hell out of that girl."

"Wow...I'm happy for you."

And Julian meant that. He played around with Pierre and Sage a lot, but the truth was that was more of his brother than a cousin. Julian couldn't count the many times he'd defended Pierre against anyone while they were growing up. Their parents used to joke that he was his personal bodyguard. They were two years apart and were really raised as brothers; they just lived in different houses.

Pierre seemed to be the overlooked cousin when he came to women. He wasn't rough with them or into games. In fact, Julian thought he'd end up dating outside of their race when he was in college, but he hadn't. Sage was a perfect fit for him and so far she seemed worthy of the position.

"You could settle down if you wanted, Jay."

Julian frowned. "How did this become about me?"

"Ever since Tes…"

"Holla at you later, cuz," Julian said, looking back down at his laptop. Pierre took the hint and left his cousin's office.

Julian hated when Pierre brought her up. He wasn't hung up on his ex, but he wasn't into rehashing old situations just because he didn't want to settle down. Pierre wasn't the only one who loved to throw Tessica King in his face.

They'd known each other all their lives; their mothers ran in the same social group. He always had a thing for her, but Tessica didn't take him seriously until the end of their sophomore year of high school. They both ended up at the same university and their romance bloomed there.

Tessica was it for Julian. He thought she felt the same until he dropped out during their sophomore year. That wasn't in Tessica's plan for her life so that meant neither was Julian anymore.

School wasn't for him, but that didn't mean he wanted to lose his girl, too. Julian had a plan and no one supported him except for Pierre. College felt like a scam to him. Dropping out allowed him to get a trade and start making real money. Construction was his way of becoming his own boss without spending tens of thousands of dollars for a piece of paper.

He'd tried to convince Tessica of that. He would still be all that he promised to be to her, but she couldn't see past the missing degree credit on his resume. She'd blocked him out of her life as soon as his withdrawal was complete. She didn't even come home after graduation. His parents told him that she'd moved to Atlanta after receiving some big job offer at a marketing firm. Julian had no choice but to move on.

He didn't move with women the way he did now just because of Tessica. She was a lesson learned, nothing more. His time was better focused on building the empire he and his cousin created than running behind a woman for anything other than entertainment.

Shaking his thoughts from his ex, Julian got back to work. He hadn't known he worked through lunch until Nicole knocked on his open door.

"I'm headed out," she announced. Julian frowned to see it was 4 in the afternoon. "You need anything before I go?"

"A date for dinner," he said, quickly. Nicole frowned. "We made plans earlier, right?"

"Right now? I thought it would be a little later."

He nodded. "No time like the present, baby."

Nicole huffed. "I guess I'm dressed for dinner."

"You are," he affirmed. "Give me about ten minutes."

Nicole smiled and nodded before walking away.

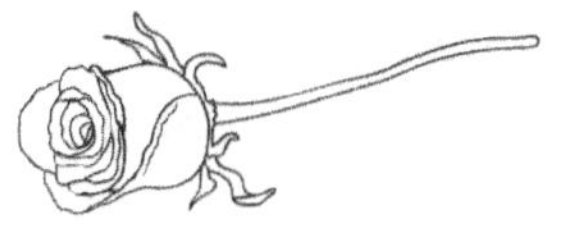

Three | Falling in Lust

Julian and Nicole drove separately to Broadway Oyster Bar once verifying that they were open for dine-in. Since it was Tuesday, there weren't many people inside. Nicole sighed as she removed her mask once they were seated. The band played a tune that reminded him of New Orleans but the chilly air of the restaurant did not.

"So was that paperwork for a city bid?" she asked. Julian nodded.

"It's looking like it's between us and two other companies."

Nicole smiled. "That's tight. Glad business is picking back up. It looked rough for a minute there."

"For real," he said, looking over the menu. "The shrimp and grits is always on time."

Nicole giggled before nodding in agreement. "And is!"

Julian rolled his eyes at her statement but kept his thoughts to himself. He noticed she did that a lot; get loud at random moments and use popular slang from social media.

"You from around here right?" he asked. Nicole frowned.

"I'm from Kansas City," she said. "I told you that."

"You tell me a lot of things," he teased.

"You saying I talk a lot, Mr. Harris?" she asked with a smirk.

"Sometimes I want you to just sit and look pretty for me." Julian licked his lips.

"I'm always sitting pretty," Nicole said. "But quiet is not my ministry." Julian had to laugh at that one. Nicole was absolutely right. When they first hired her, Julian remembered telling Pierre that he wanted to fire her because she talked too much. "I can tell you get annoyed sometimes, but that's okay. You just have to get to know me better."

"That's what we're doing now right?" Julian asked, looking Nicole up and down as his bottom lip disappeared between his teeth and slowly slid back out. Nicole blushed before shaking her head.

"A little, but getting to know each other over dinner is a little outdated and boring. We'd have to do something fun to loosen up."

"Girl, I've known you for years," Julian said. Nicole giggled.

"Not like this," she said just above a whisper. Julian caught the hint.

"What is like this?" he asked, reaching over to glide his thumb across her hand that sat on the table. She surprised him by flipping her hand over and intertwining their fingers.

"You'll see."

Julian's eyes roamed over her face, realizing how pretty she was to him. Nicole was high maintenance in a sense that she kept her appearance up. Some of her looks were a little over the top to him; he could do without the lashes, but she always looked nice. He could tell she took her time getting ready in the morning. He noticed it more when they began to date. As if she made it a point to look pretty for him. It was a thought he appreciated. Nicole's body was curvy and soft. Her stomach wasn't flat, but she was solid and presented herself well. She changed her nose ring as often as she changed the color of her hair. It was currently ginger. It went well with her lighter skin tone.

Her complexion gave way to her emotions as her face began to get red under Julian's gaze. He chuckled but decided not to mention it. "Let me taste your food."

Nicole frowned. "You lucky I like you."

"Right," he said, smirking as she cut a small piece of the fried grits patty, making sure to scoop up some shrimp and sauce with it before holding it out to him. Julian ate from her fork before winking at her.

"You ain't right," she laughed. Julian had to laugh as well.

***

After dinner, Julian realized that he wasn't ready to let go of Nicole just yet. Since they were downtown and she mentioned doing something fun, he told her they were going to Union Station and he would bring her back to her car afterward. Nicole was confused about what they were doing until they got in line for the Ferris wheel.

"Oh, I haven't been on this yet!" she said, excited. "I'm high key scared of heights though."

Julian chuckled. "So why are you excited then?" Nicole shrugged and gave him a cheeky smile. "You're crazy," he said, pulling her into his side.

"How slow does it go?" Nicole asked, looking up at the lift as they stepped up to the attendant. She used her right hand to pull the fingers on her left before opening and closing her fists.

"It'll take about 20 minutes to get up there," the attendant said. Julian pulled his wallet to pay for the tickets.

"Can we get the enclosed one?"

"Sorry...those are closed right now."

"It's a quick ride," Julian said, placing his hand on Nicole's back. She quickly looked at him while clearing her throat. Since she still had her mask on, Julian could see the fear in her eyes. Her eyebrows were almost touching and her eyes were darting back and forth.

"When we come back it'll be dark?"

"You want to go somewhere else?" he asked.

"...We came all this way. I'm just...I told you I'm scared of heights."

"My bad, I thought it was optional. I didn't know this was the only way up."

Nicole sighed. "I'm good. I can do it."

"You have to buy the tickets online," the attendant said. Julian frowned.

"Why didn't you say that?"

Nicole giggled before leading Julian out of the line. He shook his head, pulling his phone out and handing it to her. She pulled the website up, picked the tickets, and held her hand out. Julian handed her his debit card and she purchased the tickets.

Nicole laughed as they stepped back in line and showed their tickets.

"What?" Julian asked, pulling his mask off.

"When I told you that getting to know each other over dinner is boring I didn't think you listened."

He smirked, helping her up into the carousel. "Don't assume I don't."

Nicole held her hands up in surrender before scooting over to let Julian inside. The attendant lowered the bar to secure them in before patting the side of the car.

"So what do you want to know?" Julian asked. "You already know all my business."

Nicole scrunched up her face and rocked a little in a teasing manner as she took her mask off. "I do know all your business," she said. "But I want to know personal stuff."

"Ask what you want to know, love," he said, leaning back and putting his arm around the back of the seat, turning slightly to Nicole. She bit her lip in concentration before smiling.

"What's your favorite album to listen to?"

Julian's eyes widened in surprise. "Okay. I just knew you were going to ask me what my favorite color was?" Nicole laughed and shook her head. "King's Disease by Nas."

"I would not have guessed that," she said.

"Yours?"

"Don't judge me," she said. Julian smirked.

"No promises."

"Destiny Fulfilled," she said.

"I'm not shocked," he said. "You want to cater to your man, huh?"

"When I get one, yeah," she clapped back. Julian chuckled. "Favorite show?"

"I don't watch too much tv," he said. She nodded in understanding.

"My favorite show is CSI."

Julian rose an eyebrow. "You doing research?" he teased. Nicole giggled.

They begin to talk about random things as the Ferris wheel rose over downtown St. Louis. The air was a little chilly as their altitude rose, so Julian pulled Nicole into his side as they continued to talk. She sighed before snuggling into him.

"You always smell so good," she confessed. Julian chuckled while licking his bottom lip. "What is it?"

"I'm not telling you so you can tell your other dude," he teased. Nicole swatted at his chest as he laughed.

"Shut up, you know cologne mixes with your body chemistry anyway." he nodded in understanding. "I don't even talk to anyone else."

Julian decided to ignore that comment. "What's your degree in?"

"My bachelor's is in Communications and my master's is in human resources."

"You have a master's and you're working as an admin assistant?" he asked, frowning. Nicole sighed, but nodded. Julian had known she had an education, but he skipped all of those details since Pierre was the one who hired her. "What do you want to do?"

"I used to know, but with how the job market is now I'm not sure what I really want to do. You all pay well, but I definitely need to figure out my path."

Julian nodded in agreement. Nicole was in her early thirties, she definitely should have been on a career path by now. He could remember when they hired her. Pierre was excited to be able to start providing jobs for others. She was one of the first ones to respond to their job posting. Besides her flirting, she stayed on top of her work and wasn't a bother around the place.

"Let me ask you something?" he asked. Nicole stopped talking to look at him. "You feeling Pierre?"

She frowned. "No. Why would you ask me that?"

"You know you flirt a lot," he said. Nicole smirked.

"As a single woman, I like to harmlessly flirt. Pierre is in a whole relationship. Sage may not be friendly all the time, but I don't treat other women that way."

"So if he wasn't with Sage?"

Nicole rolled her eyes. "If you're trying to ask me something, Julian...just do it."

"I'm asking because I'm not into sharing with my cousin anymore."

"Those are things you ask when you get serious," Nicole stated. Julian rolled his eyes. "But to answer your question, no. I do not have feelings for Pierre like that. I never did. He's attractive. He's a great boss, but that's it," she confirmed. "I do like you though."

Julian smirked, feeling the air between them return to the playful, flirty vibe they'd had the whole evening. "You like me,

Nik?" she giggled as he muzzled his nose into her neck. Julian gently kissed her neck before playing with her fingers.

"Stop playing, you know I'm feeling you," she said. "You stay dodging me."

"I've never done that," Julian said. "I'm a busy man, baby."

Nicole rolled her eyes. "Aren't we all."

Julian chuckled, knowing Nicole wanted to argue but he decided not to take the bait. He looked around the night sky, wondering if he ever paid attention to how nice St. Louis looked at night. A few of the buildings had lights on the rooftop. He could see the Enterprise Center, the arch, and the old city hall as they slowly rounded the top of the wheel. The iridescent lights on the rooftops at different heights gave downtown a glow that they both appreciated. The sun was setting added to the ambiance of their impromptu date night.

"This is like our third time hanging out, so you know that's not true," he reiterated. Nicole nodded while staying quiet a moment. She snuggled into him more, looking around at the night sky.

"Okay," Nicole said, disturbing the calm. "Tell me an embarrassing childhood moment."

Julian laughed. He enjoyed getting to know Nicole. She asked very random questions and seemed invested in his answers. He usually didn't divulge all of his personal business, but he would oblige her. Even if it was only for tonight.

***

Nicole was at her desk the next morning looking unusually pretty. Her appearance was always top tier to Julian, but he was confident the glow she had was his doing. He licked his lips as he walked off the elevator towards her, watching her eyes briefly light up at the sight in front of her.

"You grinning for me or these?" he asked, raising the bouquet of flowers up a little. Nicole blushed.

"Depends on if those are for me?" she asked, leaning over on her desk with her arms crossed under her chest. Julian smirked at the picture she painted.

"Who else would they be for, love?" He chuckled as she squealed, standing up to round the desk.

"In that case, the grin was for you and the flowers," she giggled, taking them from him as she leaned back against the desk and moved the bouquet to her nose. Julian watched her inhale slowly a few times before her eyelashes fluttered and she looked back up at him sweetly. "Thank you, Mr. Harris," she teased.

Julian smiled. "Cut it out."

Nicole laughed before looking around. "I have to find something to put these in. You are so sweet."

He shrugged it off. "I had fun with you last night. Just wanted to show you that."

Nicole's grin turned into a more seductive look that made Julian shake his head to rid him of the thoughts he had. "I appreciate that. Can I show you later?"

"You two need to stop."

Julian rolled his eyes as Nicole jumped at the sound of Pierre's voice as he came out of the breakroom. Instead of responding, Julian walked off towards his own office. Pierre followed.

"You got everything ready for the party?" Pierre asked, circling his desk that was almost identical to Pierre's, just with a different metal finish.

Julian sighed as he plopped down in the leather chair on the other side of Pierre's desk. "Just about. Worried about this menu. Trying not to do buffet style but it was the most cost effective."

"They have servers though, right?"

Julian nodded. "Supposed to have the barriers in front of the food and the servers will have masks and gloves."

"It'll be cool. Checking temps at the door and making sure some sanitizer is everywhere." They both laughed. "Times are crazy."

Julian had to agree. What seemed like a short-term virus was beginning to look like the world's new normal. Julian didn't so much mind the mask, he realized. He liked being able to move around conspicuously. Especially if he had a hat or hoodie on, no one could recognize him unless he wanted them to. People in stores and public places weren't particularly chatting and got right to the point. That was how Julian operated and he appreciated the same in others. However, he didn't like the impending threat that covid had on everything he did now. He always kept his circle small, but now it seemed outside of his family the only person he was comfortably around was Nicole.

"So y'all went out last night?" Pierre asked. Julian looked at his cousin and realized he had zoned out. He nodded, hoping Pierre wouldn't ask too many questions. "You serious about her?"

"I'm not serious about anything but work," he answered, quickly. Pierre shook his head.

"Bro…"

"Don't even start, old man."

"I'm 29 and you're a year younger than me," Pierre said. "Stop calling me old for I knock you out."

Julian chuckled, deciding not to press his cousin's buttons that morning. "Don't trip off me and Nicole. We just coolin'."

"She ain't just coolin'," Pierre said, shaking his head but waving his cousin off. Julian's mind went to the promise of seeing her again tonight so he got up to leave his cousin's office and go back to Nicole's desk.

"Hey pretty lady," he said, sneaking up on her. She jumped and he laughed.

"Why you play so much?" she asked, trying to sound mad but smiling at his presence anyway.

"What you doing?" he asked, running his hand down the length of her arm. Her back arched a little as she pushed her chair around to face him.

"Editing the report for the shareholders."

Julian nodded before leaning over, putting both of his hands on the arms of her chair and running his nose over her neck.

"You smell good."

Nicole sat up straighter, moving closer to him. "Um, you like it?" Julian nodded before pecking her neck and moving to stand back up. She followed him with hooded eyes.

"What is it?"

"Coach."

He nodded. "So tonight?"

Nicole smiled. "My place. 8 okay? I have some things to do after work. My mom wants me to…"

Julian frowned. "You don't have to explain to me. I'll be there at 8."

Nicole gave him a closed-mouth smile. "Good."

She squealed as Julian spun her chair around to face her computer screen again. "Now get back to work."

Julian walked away as he heard her laugh. He didn't see her for the rest of the day, but he didn't mind knowing they'd be spending the night together. Pierre left for the day before him as well, so he was left to lock up on his way out around 5. Knowing he had some hours to kill, Julian went to his parents' house to see what they were up to. To his surprise and satisfaction, only his mom was home.

"There's my favorite son," Joyce said. Julian laughed as he hugged her and kissed her forehead.

"Hey Momma, what you doing home alone?"

"Your sister is at work and that husband of mine is at Lowe's again."

Julian laughed at how she rolled her eyes. “What he working on now?”

“I didn’t even ask,” she said, rolling her eyes. “How was your day?”

“It wasn’t too much going on today.”

“Everything on the up and up?” she asked as she usually did. Julian smiled and told her that it was.

Although Joyce was proud of her son and nephew, the entrepreneur's life made her extremely nervous. She was used to the men in her family working for someone else at a steady job like her father and husband had done her whole life. Joyce had been the biggest champion for him getting a higher education. He knew she was beyond disappointed when he decided to drop out and even more scared when he and Pierre started their company. It wasn’t until he had been moved out for at least six months that she realized the company was profitable enough to support Pierre and Julian that she eased up a little.

That didn’t stop her from worrying from time to time.

“You staying for dinner?” she asked while flipping through channels on the wall-mounted tv.

“No ma’am, I got plans.”

“Um hum,” she mumbled. He laughed.

“Momma, why you doing all that?”

“When you going to settle down, baby? I don’t like you doing too much with all these women.”

“Who told you I had a lot of women?” he asked, trying not to laugh. “I’m chilling, Momma.”

“You too old to be chilling,” she said, dropping the remote at her side to look at her son. “I would like to dance with you at a wedding before I’m too old to dance.”

Julian frowned. “That’ll be a while. I like the bachelor life.”

Joyce rolled her eyes before turning back to the tv. “Um hum… mess around and be the last bachelor left.”

Julian chuckled, but he was completely over the conversation. Ever since Pierre got serious with Sage, their family had been down Julian's neck about him doing the same. He didn't want to keep her going, so he let her last statement go unanswered and just put his attention on whatever she was watching.

***

Dinner at Nicole's was good as usual. This was one of the reasons Julian liked spending time with her. She could cook and didn't mind doing so for him. It was rare nowadays for women and he appreciated not having to eat out all the time.

He was currently spread out next to her on her bed, full from his meal, watching the highlights from college football.

"You came over here to watch ESPN?" Nicole snapped. "You're boring."

"I'm at your place," he said. "You're supposed to entertain me."

"I fed you already. This ain't a free show," she teased. Julian eyed her before she started laughing. "I'm playing boo, but I would like your attention," she said, pushing all of her weight onto him. He licked his lips and bent his left leg, causing his basketball shorts to slip over his knee and down to his thigh. His hand massaged the back of Nicole's neck while they looked into each other's eyes. Hers fluttered closed as she dropped her head to his shoulder and he kissed her temple. Nicole sighed as both his hands slid down her back and he caressed her butt.

"Julian," she breathed. He rubbed it for a minute before squeezing it, causing their bodies to mesh more.

"Yes, love?"

"..."

Nicole turned her head to try and talk but his tongue stopped her. She groaned into the kiss before gripping his shoulders and kissing him harder. He nibbled on her bottom lip from right to left as he always did before squeezing her butt again. This time Nicole felt him rise through his shorts. She shivered as he moved her around to feel it better.

"I want you," he said. "Bad."

"You do?" she breathed. He nodded against her neck.

"Can I have you?"

Nicole didn't respond. She wanted to ask him what they were to each other first, but her body was beating up her mind at that moment. Nodding to herself, Nicole tried to push her palms into the bed and move off of him, but all Julian did was flip them over, run his hands up to both of her breasts, and kissed her again.

"Julian stop," Nicole moaned loudly. He nodded.

"I am," he lied. She shivered as his fingertips greedily pushed further into her flesh.

"No, you aren't."

"That's you, love." Nicole felt her arch into his touch and wondered if he was right. She opened her eyes to see his hands move back and under her shirt. She shivered when he pushed past her sports bra and felt her flesh.

"That's you though!" she laughed. Julian looked up at her and smiled before biting his lip.

"It's your fault," he mumbled. Nicole felt weaker as his voice got deeper.

"How?"

He pushed her shirt up and pulled the bra to the side. "Your skin is too soft."

Nicole couldn't laugh if she wanted to as he rubbed his lips against her nipple a few times before taking it into his mouth. She was about to say bye to her little declaration and pull her clothes out of his way but his phone went off. Nicole tried to catch her breath as Julian kissed the skin above her heart before pulling the bra and shirt down. Nicole calmed her nerves as Julian took the call, she listened attentively until she heard him address his dad. Relaxing, she decided to go into the living room to risk temptation again.

Julian came in a few minutes later, leaning over to kiss her.

"Everything okay?" she asked.

"Party stuff," he said, looking over her. "Why you come in here?"

She sighed. "It was getting late…I figured you'd be leaving soon."

Julian slowly nodded. "Alright…walk me out."

Timidly, Nicole walked him to the front door, wondering if he was upset about them not having sex. She relaxed when he turned to kiss her before leaving.

"See you in the morning?" he asked.

Nicole smiled. "I do work there," she teased. Julian playfully rolled his eyes before stepping down out of the doorway.

"Lock the door and goodnight, smartass."

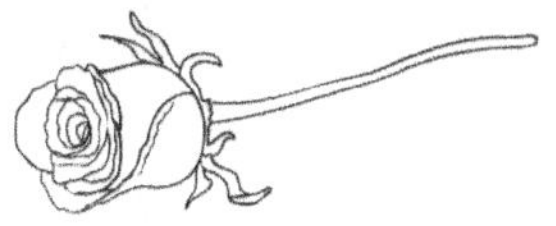

Four | A Love Like This

Joyce and Ray's anniversary party was being held at Windows on Washington. Julian reserved a space for only 40 people to be seated comfortably and socially distant from each round table. He hired an event planner who created an elegant setting at his parents' request. There were long white curtains draped around three of the walls of the space, leaving the windows clear for the view. A soft blue light was placed at the bottom of each curtain to illuminate the silver, blue and white decor. The guests of honor had a sweetheart table right in front of the dance floor and stage. The catered meal would be served to eliminate contamination from a buffet-style dinner.

"It's rare people get to dress up nowadays," Joyce said. "We needed a night to step out."

Julian opted out of a suit, but the suspenders and bow tie he paired with his dark blue slacks still kept in the after 5, semi-formal theme. He arrived at the venue a little early while checking on his parent's ride for the night.

"What? No date?"

Julian rolled his eyes at the annoying sound of his little sister's voice.

"Shut up, Niecey," he looked over her attire and approved of the dark blue, long sleeve dress she wore. "You look nice."

Niecey gasped. "My brother is giving me a compliment? Are you sick?" Julian rolled his eyes before pulling her mask off and throwing it on the floor. She rolled her eyes. "You are so childish. You lucky I have another one," she said, holding her sparkling silver clutch up in the air. Julian shrugged his shoulders before heading into the ballroom.

"You don't have a date?" he asked. "I thought you said you were bringing someone?"

"They're meeting me here," she said. Julian nodded. "Everything good?"

"No thanks to you."

Deniece sighed before waving his obvious attitude with her off. "Everything looks good. Calm down and relax. It's party time."

Julian shook his head before walking towards the stage. The DJ was set up and ready to go. He looked at his watch and saw they had about 15 minutes before the start time on the invitation. Their parents would be arriving in 30 minutes.

"Right now you can play what you want," he instructed. "I don't want you to start on the list until they get here."

The DJ nodded before giving him a thumbs up. Julian tapped the table before walking off the stage. He smiled when Sage and Pierre came through the double doors, taking off their masks.

"We came early just in case you needed us," Pierre said, hugging his cousin. Julian side-hugged Sage before complimenting her appearance.

"We're all good, just waiting on the guests of honor."

Pierre nodded. "Momma said the limo just got to their house." Julian sighed in relief. "They'll be on time."

"Bet," Julian said. "Come with me to get a drink."

"I'm going to check my makeup," Sage said, leaving the cousins to go to the bar alone. While taking a moment to relax at the bar, Julian watched the door while his parents' friends and some family began to file in sporadically. He made mental notes on his RSVP list, smiling at the faces he knew that his parents would truly appreciate.

"It looks dope in here. This was all your idea?" Pierre asked.

"Shut up, I hired somebody."

Pierre laughed. "I know that. I meant the colors and stuff."

Julian shrugged. "The 40th anniversary is the ruby anniversary so I just kind of based it off that."

"I see you cuz," Pierre teased. Julian laughed but looked around, feeling accomplished. He'd chosen wine burgundy and champagne as the color scheme. That was really all he'd given the event planner, but she ran with it and did a good job. There were ruby gems on the tables with tall centerpieces that held champagne-colored roses on each table. The balloon garlands were full and elegant and fit the decor of the room perfectly. He was almost upset that he hadn't been there earlier to offer more thanks, but he would definitely leave her a raving review.

"Is that Norma and Von?" Pierre asked. "I thought they got divorced."

Pierre chuckled, looking at the pair as they walked in. "They did."

"Oh wow." The cousins laughed as Sage and Deniece walked over to them.

"They just pulled up," Deniece said. Julian nodded before he finished his drink and stood up. He and his sister walked out of the ballroom and towards the elevator so they could escort them in.

Ray Harris was short in stature but made up for it in heart. He used to be heavier, but a recent health scare caused him to take on a pescatarian lifestyle. He'd leaned out and gotten a little more muscular, turning back the hands of time in his face. Ray was a proud member of the bald, bearded club, keeping his facial hair trimmed at the length his wife loved. His dark skin held a warm undertone that could be felt by the ones around him. He was a man who showed his love for his family in many ways, not afraid to share his emotions. Joyce was just about his height but loved to joke that she was taller than her husband. Her almond-colored skin held very few wrinkles outside of a small cut under her eye from a childhood accident. Her green eyes were her main feature, sparkling each time she smiled. Joyce loved to change her hair up but had fallen for a full gray feathered bob in the last few years.

Julian nodded at Deniece, who was in charge of putting their outfits for the evening together. She smiled knowingly at his silent approval. Joyce had on a satin, champagne gown that had jewels going over the sleeves and around the waist. Ray's suit was champagne with wine pinstripes. Julian was sure the hat was all his own doing.

"Ain't no way you two been alive 40 years let alone married that long," Julian said, kissing his mother's cheek first before hugging his father.

"You better get into it," Joyce said, posing. Julian frowned before Deniece laughed.

"Stop teaching her slang," Julian teased, pushing his sister's arm as she walked around to their father.

"She teaches me," Deniece said, kissing her father's cheek. "You look handsome, Daddy."

"Thank you, baby girl," he said, pushing his son over to Joyce's side. "Let's get this party started."

Julian looked at the banquet hall door at Pierre and nodded. Pierre nodded as well before he pointed towards the Dj and he and Sage moved out of the way.

"Alright now, the guests of honor have arrived. I need everyone on your feet to welcome Ray and Joyce Harris to their 40th anniversary party!"

Everyone stood and clapped as they walked in when "Love Ballad" by L.T.D began to play. Deniece and Julian escorted their parents to the middle of the dance floor before going to the table they were seated at. Julian smiled as Ray pulled Joyce to him by her waist. Joyce blushed as she put both of her hands on his face, kissing him before wrapping her arms around his neck.

"Alright now, don't hurt her, Mr. Ray!" the DJ said. Everyone cheered as they began to sway together.

"I said I wasn't going to cry tonight," Deniece said. Julian chuckled before elbowing her.

"Tighten up, sis."

Deniece rolled her eyes before wrapping her arm around her brother's waist as they watched their parents dance. "You did good with the party, bro."

"Your mom is gorgeous!" Sage said, next to them. "Like seriously."

The Dj invited other couples to dance. Pierre placed his hand on the small of Sage's back and guided her out to the dance floor. Julian and Deniece settled in their seats as Jaren and Janet left the table as well.

"We lame," Deniece joked.

"Speak for yourself," Julian said. "I could have had a date."

He did think of inviting Nicole to the party but didn't want the interrogation of who she was to him from his family. They weren't serious and he didn't need that type of pressure. Plus, he wanted to make sure his focus was on his parents enjoying their party.

And enjoy it, they did. The Dj make sure to mix in a lot of old and new school. Julian was proud that most of the night, no one was sitting down. Pierre had made a slide show of Ray and Joyce's marriage over the years that played against a projector in a wall while they had dinner, but after that it was back to the party.

"My feet hurt a little," Sage whined. "But I'm having so much fun."

"You want your slides out of the car?" Pierre asked. Sage smiled but shook her head.

"No, I'm okay baby."

"My nephew is so in love," Joyce said. "Who would have thought?"

"And Sage is such a sweetheart," Janet chimed in. Sage thanked her and Julian chuckled.

"She ain't as sweet as y'all think," he teased. Sage sucked her teeth before swatting at his arm. "See."

"That's because you teasing her," Joyce said. "Son, you need to take a page from your cousin's book and settle down."

"Oh hell," Pierre mumbled. Sage giggled before cuddling into his side.

"I will when the right one comes along."

"What does that even mean?" Ray said. "Your momma ran up on me."

"Stop telling that lie all these years!" Joyce said. The whole table laughed.

Julian frowned as Deniece shuffled over to him with her eyebrows pushed together and her bottom lip between her teeth.

"So...I knew Tess would be in town and I invited her," she spoke fast. Julian frowned, opening his mouth to speak but she cut him off. "And I didn't tell you until now and she just got off the elevator so be nice."

"Is that little Tessica King?" Julian heard his mother on the other side of the round table. "Look at you!"

"Happy anniversary, Mr. and Mrs. Harris."

Julian closed his eyes. It had been well over a decade since he'd heard that silky tone of her voice. He immediately regretted it; all of the moments he heard that same tone proclaim love for him flooded back to his memory. Deniece kept a close eye on him, obviously waiting for some type of reaction. He was frozen, internally battling with the need to lay eyes on her and the desire to walk away before he could. Julian honestly didn't know what to do at that very moment.

"I could only aspire to be in love for 40 years," she said. "You two truly are a blessing to everyone who knows you."

"Aw, just as sweet as ever. You'll get there with that husband of yours," Joyce said.

"Unfortunately, we divorced about a year ago," Tessica said. "But all is well."

Julian groaned hearing that his former love was now single. He quickly stood up, making his way back towards the open bar. Pierre stopped him on his journey.

"Is that Tess?" Pierre asked. Julian looked up at his cousin with a dead stare.

"You know it is," he said. "Deniece invited her without even telling me."

"You know how Auntie feels about her," Pierre said.

"So what? When I broke it off with her, they should have, too!"

Pierre snickered. "She's the one who broke it off."

Julian pushed Pierre away from him before ordering another shot. He knew more alcohol wasn't the rational thing to do but at the moment he didn't care. He had handled all of his party duties and was on the verge of calling Nicole for a nightcap. His parents were having a good time, the party turned out great. He didn't want to ruin his night by arguing with Tessica.

However, looking at her from across the room made Julian realize that was all he wanted to do.

Julian put his shot glass down on the bar and quickly walked back over to the table. He cut off whatever Tessica was saying to Deniece by slowly pulling her chair back. She gasped in shock before looking up at him.

"Bro, what are you doing?" Deniece said. Julian ignored her and grabbed Tessica's hand.

"Let me talk to you for a minute," he more so stated than asked. Tessica sighed as Julian pulled her from the chair and began to walk to the ballroom exit. Once out in the hallway, Julian dropped her hand. "What are you doing here?"

Tessica raised an eyebrow. "Niecey invited me. She didn't tell you?"

"You know what I mean. What are you *doing* here?"

Tessica cleared her throat before her shoulders dropped. "You know I always admired your parents' marriage. I had to come celebrate them...I also wanted to see you."

"See me for what, Tessica?" he asked, exhaling from his nose. "We don't have no business with each other."

She bit her lip before pushing her hands together in a praying motion. "I realize you're still mad about what happened with us."

"I'm not," he lied. "I'm over you leaving me like I wasn't shit."

Tessica exhaled deeply before dropping her hands to her side. Julian wanted to groan from the thump in his heart as he looked at her hips. "Are you going to let me talk? You pulled me out here for an explanation, right?" Julian gave her a blank stare. "I've been thinking about you...about us for a while now and I...I messed up, Ju."

Julian's head began to pound. There was no way that Tessica King was standing here, more than a decade after leaving him, saying this.

"Yo, you can really leave," Julian said, cutting Tessica's apology off.

"Really?" she asked, frowning as she crossed her arms under her breasts. "For real, Julian?"

"For real, Tessica," he said, backing up a little to not smell the Baccarat Rouge 540 he knew she was wearing. "I don't even know why you thought you could show up here and expect me to talk to you like this."

"You're the one who pulled me out here."

"Don't act like you didn't show up here for more than my parents," he laughed. "You out your mind."

Before she could say anything else, Julian turned and went back into the ballroom. He went to look for Pierre to ask him for a ride to Nicole's since he was sober enough to know he shouldn't drive. He rolled his eyes when Deniece stopped him.

"Where's Tessica?"

"Where's Pierre?"

"...He left with Sage a few minutes ago."

Julian silently cursed before pulling his phone out as he went to find his parents. He called Nicole and she answered on the third ring.

"Party over?" she asked. "How'd it go?"

"You mind coming to get me. I don't need to drive."

"Your family not there to take you home?" she asked.

"I don't want to go home," he said. "I'm trying to stay with you."

Nicole sighed. "You'd have to give me a second. I was already in bed."

"Whenever you get here is cool. Just let me know when you're close so I can be downstairs."

"Okay."

Julian hung up his phone as he found his parents packing up their gifts. "Niecey got that. You two enjoy yourselves."

"I'm old and sleepy, son," Ray said. "It's time for these old bones to get in the bed."

Joyce laughed. "We had so much fun though. Thank you, son, this was very nice."

"You know your kids had to show out for you," he said. Joyce gave him a knowing smile.

"We know who did what," she said. Julian just nodded, not having to sell his sister out. "Who are you riding with? You bet not drive."

"I'm not, ma'am. I can walk you two out though."

"Did you talk with Tessica?" Joyce asked as she wrapped her hands around his arm. Julian sighed.

"We don't have anything to talk about, Momma."

"She seems really sincere," Joyce urged. "You know I always loved you two together."

"So did I," Julian mumbled.

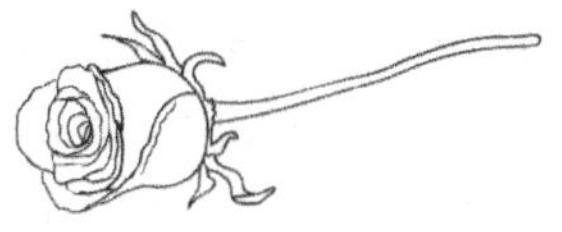

Five | Young Love

8 years ago

Higher education was a scam. That was all Julian Harris could think as he sat at his desk in his single dorm room, pulling at the ends of his braids. His scalp itched and his hair was unkempt but that only reminded him that he canceled on his braider to finish this paper that was due in 2 hours. His microeconomics class made him want to roll up after every session and he wasn't even a smoker. It was almost as if the material covered in class was never a topic of discussion when it came to assignments and exams. That on top of the ridiculous amount of money it cost just to breathe on campus made him want to quit.

If he was honest with himself, every class made him feel that way. Julian wasn't college material. It wasn't that he wasn't smart, he just didn't see the point in having a degree. The only reason he even enrolled was due to pressure from his family when his cousin, Pierre, decided to go to Texas Southern. They were raised as close as brothers and the expectations on them to be excellent were equally yoked. Julian opted for a school close to home...and close to Tessica.

Thinking about his baby was second nature to him. The typical high school sweetheart story with a little encouragement from both of their parents made falling in love easy. They had always been friends who harmlessly flirted, but ever since she asked him to be her escort at her debutante ball, their fate was sealed.

Tessica King was Julian's heart. Even sitting at his desk all he could think about were her full lips, caramel skin, and wide, pretty eyes. Everything about her complimented him. In heels, she was the perfect height for him to look down and kiss her without straining his back. Her curvy body fit in his arms without resistance. Her calming temperament eased his aggression. The Belle to his Beast; Julian was only sure of one thing in life and that was eventually making her Tessica Harris.

He smirked before sitting back to distance himself from his laptop screen as he Facetimed her. She answered right after the first ring with a pout. He licked his lips, the light from her screen illuminating her face in a way that made his decision to call her a good one. The red undertones of her skin lit a fire inside of him.

"I know you aren't done with that paper, Juju."

He licked his lips. "Come help me."

"I'm not walking across campus this late," she giggled.

"I'll come to you," he persisted. Tessica rolled her eyes but fought to hide her smile. "You know you want to cuddle."

"No, I want you to finish your paper," she said, pointing a finger at him. "...and then I want to cuddle."

Julian chuckled as her laughter filled his heart. "I'll be over there in a minute. Do you want anything?"

"No," she smiled. "I'm okay. See you when you get here."

Julian hurried with the process of packing his Adidas gym bag for an overnight stay. After throwing some clothes and sneakers inside, he placed his laptop and charger on top before zipping it up. Putting his slides on and grabbing his wallet and keys, he locked up his door and headed to the parking lot. Tessica's off-campus apartment was a 10-minute drive from his dorm. When he pulled his 2005 Chevy Impala into the spot next to her 2008 Lexus ES 350, he frowned to see her standing in her screen door. He hated that she was on the first floor of the building.

"Why are you outside, love?" he said while pulling his bag out of the backseat.

"I was waiting for my man," she teased.

"You know better," he said, opening the screen door and pulling her in for a kiss. The way she melted into him almost made him forget his current annoyance. "Don't stand out here like that. It's too late at night for that."

"Hush," she said, turning to fully let him inside. "I just opened the door a minute ago."

"I missed you," he said, kissing her again after locking her front door. Tessica giggled before wrapping her arms around his neck.

"I was just with you before work," she said. He gave her a dead stare and she laughed. "I missed you, too. Now get to work. You have an hour to finish that paper."

Julian sighed as Tessica walked away, her hips begging to take his attention away from his studies. He would much rather interrupt whatever Tessica was watching on television in her bedroom. He thought about just tanking his assignment but knew that she would have something to say.

Outside of his family's influence, Tessica was also very adamant about higher education. She had their whole future pretty much planned out. After graduation, she would apply to graduate school and Julian would start his business. She hinted at wanting to be engaged by that time. Julian was down with that plan.

He sat down at her small, round dining room table and pulled his laptop out of his bag. It only took 30 minutes for him to finally give up and turn in whatever he had. At least he'd get some credit for that. After turning his laptop off, Julian grabbed a pair of boxers and socks out of his bag and headed to the bathroom. Taking a quick shower, he walked into her bedroom to see her securing a scarf around her pressed hair that was now wrapped around her head.

"You're done?" she asked. Julian nodded before climbing into bed and pushing her decorative pillows off. Tessica giggled as he pulled her soft body into his. She sighed as he kissed her lips. Quick, passionate kisses relaxed her body as she rubbed his neck.

"You know I have an early class," she mumbled against his lips. Julian groaned, causing her to giggle. "Julian, you know how you get. I can't be up all night with you and be tired during Media law."

"We'll cross that bridge when we get there," he said, pushing his fingertips into the meat between the back of her thigh and the curve of her butt. Tessica groaned as he pulled her leg around his waist.

"You make me sick," she said, showing her surrender by sitting up and pulling her nightgown off. Julian just licked his lips as he laid fully on his back, watching his woman straddle his waist.

With only a few weeks left in the semester, Julian finally decided that school really wasn't for him. Today was the deadline to sign up for next semester's classes and he opted out. He hadn't told anyone about his decision to leave school. In fact, he'd even gone so far as to let Tessica help him pick out classes as if he would enroll. He felt bad about lying to her, but Julian didn't even want to bring it up to her until he was sure. He wanted to tell her before he told his parents, but the first person who had to know was Pierre.

Julian called him as he pulled out of the parking lot of the student center.

"I did it," Julian said. "I'm dropping out."

"Hold on bro. I don't think I heard you right."

Julian chuckled. "I said I dropped out after this semester. I missed the deadline to enroll."

"It's today, right? You still have time."

Julian realized his cousin thought it was a mistake. "No, P. I did it on purpose."

"You did what?" Pierre asked his cousin.

"You heard what I said, P."

"Nah...I don't think I did." Pierre adjusted his phone on whatever it was leaning against to get closer to the screen. He frowned, looking over his cousin's face to see if he was actually serious or not.

Julian sighed. Out of all the people in his life, he thought Pierre would be the one to support his decision to quit school.

"I didn't have a choice."

Pierre chuckled. "You tell Aunt Joyce and Uncle Ray yet?" Julian ran his hand down his face. "Oh, please let me come with you to tell them! I have to see this. They gonna kill you. Don't tell them until I get home for Christmas break."

"It's not like it was their money," he said. It was true that Julian funded his education through grants, scholarships, and student loans.

"You think that matters?" Pierre frowned, standing up straight. "All we've heard since we were kids is higher education. Our parents never even gave us an option not to go to school." Julian looked at Pierre, waiting for him to finish. "Ju..."

"I got a plan, bro," Julian said. "Hear me out."

Pierre sighed, trusting his cousin wouldn't change the trajectory of his life on a whim. "What's the plan?"

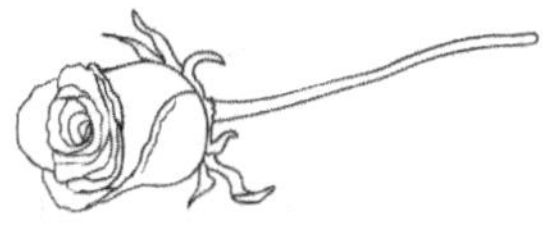

Six | Redemption's on Your Mind

Walking out of the gym a week after his parents' anniversary, Julian felt the effects of partying and drinking the previous week.

"You letting that age catch up to you?" Pierre asked, swatting at Julian's chest. "A little shaky in there huh?"

Julian rolled his eyes. "Keep playing like you ain't older than me."

Pierre's laugh was cut short as they walked towards their cars in the parking lot. They met up at the gym this time instead of riding together. Julian followed his cousin's gaze to his truck and sucked his teeth.

"You gotta be kidding me," he said, looking over Tessica's slim frame as she leaned casually against the grill. "Get off my truck."

Tessica frowned. "You don't have to be rude, Ju…Hi, Pierre."

"Tessica," he said, short and polite before looking at his cousin. "I'm out."

"Bro!" Julian said. Pierre shook his head before walking past the truck to his own car. Tessica bit her lip before standing up straight, waiting to see if Julian would say anything else.

He had to admit that time had been good to her. Although she had thinned out, her hips still curved in whatever she wore. A complete contrast to the elegant style he'd seen her in just last week, Tessica had her hair pulled into a messy bun, giving her cheekbones and pretty eyes a nice display. She looked runway ready, even in a pair of distressed jeans, a simple white blouse, and olive green heeled combat boots.

"You look nice," he said before he could catch himself. Her shock and surprise did not go unnoticed.

"Thank you." Her smile made him take his instant regret back. "...can we talk for real this time?"

"I said you look nice," Julian said. "Not that I wanted to talk to you."

He couldn't help but laugh as Tessica's jaw dropped. He hit the unlock button on his key fob, walked around her, opened his back door, and threw his gym bag in. She had pivoted to watch him but stayed in the same spot. Julian sighed.

"Get in," he said, nodding to the passenger seat. Tessica nodded before walking around to hop in the truck. Julian ran his hand down his face before getting into the driver's seat. Tessica frowned when he didn't move to do anything else.

"Why aren't you starting the truck?"

"We aren't going anywhere. Talk."

Tessica smoothed her hands over her jeans before looking over Julian's face. It bothered him that she still made his heart pump a little faster just by doing so.

"First...how are you?" she asked in a tone so soft it unarmed him.

"Why'd your marriage fail, Tess?" He asked, getting comfortable in his seat.

She pushed her back against the door and crossed her arms under her breast. "Seriously?"

"You wanted to talk," he said with a sly grin. "Never said what we'd talk about."

"Do we have to talk about that?"

"Hell yeah," he said, frowning. "You thought I wasn't gonna ask? You want to talk about the past and apologize, I want to know what happened that was so bad you came back like that."

Tessica huffed. "You can not be so smug about it."

He ran his hand down his fade before shaking his head. "Tess, love...you don't have room to request anything from me."

Julian eyed her while she pulled at her right index finger with her left hand. Julian wanted to laugh. She had been doing that since they were kids. Whenever she was nervous, Tessica tried to pop her knuckles, even though she didn't like the feeling. Julian leaned over and pulled her finger out of her hand. Tessica looked up at him and scrunched her nose.

"On paper, it was a good marriage. It was decent," she said. "Mommy and Daddy loved him, he was a successful lawyer. We both were in the Divine 9. It was perfect."

"Get to the part I care about," he said.

Tessica grinned. "Oh, you care now?" Julian rolled his eyes. Tessica giggled before waving off the playful moment. "There was no passion there. No real connection," she looked up into his eyes. "Not like we were."

"When did you meet him?"

"Julian, why does that matter?"

"Was it before or after I dropped out?"

She looked down at her hand and Julian wanted to put her out of his car. "I met him before...but we didn't start dating until after."

"How soon after?"

Tessica signed. "Is there a point to this?"

"You want me to entertain this bullshit ass conversation, Tess. Answer the questions or stop talking."

She blinked a few times before nodding. "I think I'm done talking."

Julian shrugged and hit the unlock button on the door handle. He watched as Tessica jumped down to the ground and quickly walked over to her Cadillac. Julian sucked his teeth as he waited for her to pull off. Pierre was calling him as he pulled out of the gym's parking lot.

"You good?" he asked.

Julian sighed. "I tried to be cool about it," he admitted. "She gets under my skin."

"That's because you ain't let go of that broken heart."

Julian rolled his eyes. "I been over that."

Pierre chuckled. "You asked her when she started messing with her husband didn't you?"

"...Ex husband."

Pierre laughed fully this time. "I know you like the back of my hand, bro. You still love her after all this time?"

"P...it's Tessica."

"Yeah, I know who it is. She's the one who left you high and dry when you didn't fit into her perfect little box of what success looked like. Don't let that innocent, sorry act trap you, Julian. She left for a reason and she's back for a reason."

Julian hadn't even thought about a motive other than the one she tried to sell him. How long had she even been divorced? Was it even final? Now he had more questions than he did when he saw her the other night at the party. He groaned, hating the feeling of confusion.

Julian would be lying to himself if he said he never had moments where he wanted Tessica by his side. That has always been his plan. He may have been outside as far as dating now, but when he was younger, Tessica was it. He was teased relentlessly by his boys about how in love he was, but it was hard not to be.

They'd known each other too well before they even started dating. It made it that much easier to fall in love without caution. Outside of Pierre, Tessica was his best friend. Julian never thought she would drop him the way she did. He may have been more upset with himself.

"You can't put nothing past nobody," he mumbled.

Pierre sighed. "I know you want to figure out what she's doing home, but think about this for real, Ju," he warned. "Be careful with her.

"I hear you, bro," Julian said. They got off the phone as Julian focused on driving home and tried not to focus on Tessica.

And if it wasn't one thing it was another, especially when it came to running a business.

"I hate this building, yo," Julian said as he shook his head, leaning against the hood of his truck next to Pierre. They sat a street down from their office, looking at the water gushing from the sewers as the first responders worked quickly to contain the burst.

"How does a water pipe burst and it's not even that cold?" Pierre asked, frustration showing through the frown on his face. "It's literally in the 50s."

"We just need to find a space in a plaza or something to buy."

"Yeah, but in the meantime?"

"We work from home until they get this together," Pierre said. "Call Nicole."

Julian sighed. He hadn't talked to Nicole since the night of his parents' party. They had sent a few messages, but nothing of substance and he could tell that she was irritated.

"You call her," Julian said. Pierre looked at his cousin and laughed.

"Really, Ju?"

"I don't feel like all that right now," he admitted. "Hurry up before she drives to work."

Pierre sighed but pulled out his phone as they both went to their respective cars and got in.

Julian really didn't have anything pressing for the day, so he decided to go visit his parents. He knew they'd had a tough time adjusting to being alone when the pandemic first hit. Although he had been on his own for some years now, Deniece just moved out and as empty nesters, Joyce and Ray had to learn how to be alone again. His mom was more social than his dad, so staying in all the time with little to no contact with the outside world was driving her crazy. Julian taught them how to Facetime, but Joyce absolutely hated it. She said she'd rather see her kids.

A few months ago, Deniece moved back home due to financial issues. Her job had furloughed her during Covid and she hadn't been called back yet. Julian loved his little sister, but she was annoying to him. Deniece was the kid who did "everything right" in their parents' eyes. She actually graduated with a degree. She didn't use it though, so Julian didn't see how her accolades even compared to him running a successful business.

His parents had a nice home in Lake St. Louis. It was a two-story home with a two-car garage attached. There was a light gray brick foundation that was about waist-high all around with the rest of the home covered in ash blue siding. It was trimmed in white with a tan siding at the top of the first garage and the second floor main window. The first garage sat ahead of the second one with the curved walkway to the front porch on the right side of it. Next to the front door was a big, bay window that overlooked the living room. The backyard was large enough for a family pool, but Joyce never wanted one.

They purchased it when Julian was just entering high school. He could remember how proud his dad was when Joyce ran through the house crying and praising God. She'd spent months decorating it before she would even sleep in it.

"I can't sleep in here until it's complete," she kept telling her husband when he was tired of staying with her parents.

Julian pulled his truck in front of the garage next to Deniece's Honda. He used his key to unlock the front door. His baby sister was laid out on the couch watching reality tv. She looked back at him and rolled his eyes.

"Go back to work," he said, swatting at her head.

"Momma, get your son!" Deniece yelled towards the kitchen. Julian chuckled before heading that way. He smiled to see his mom cutting up potatoes on the marble island.

"Why are you always bothering her?"

"It's fun," he said while going to wash his hands.

"Why aren't you at work?"

"Some pipes burst on Washington and the road is closed."

"What?" she asked, frowning. "It's always something. Give me another potato then."

"You're frying them?" he asked. Joyce smirked.

"Yes, son." Julian nodded before going to the pantry and pulling two potatoes out. He went back to the sink, rinsed them off, and then handed them to his mother. She laughed. "Just greedy."

"You know I love your fried potatoes."

"I can't wait to pass my recipe to your wife one day," she teased. Julian fought hard not to roll his eyes, knowing he would get hit for it.

"Can we not do this today, Ma?"

"Tessica's mom called me," she ignored his wish. "Said she moved back?"

Julian sighed heavily. "Apparently."

"Did you let her explain herself?" Joyce asked, eyeing her son as he rounded the island to sit on a barstool.

"If it was the other way around would y'all ask that to her?"

"She's not my child, you are."

Julian sighed. "I don't know, Ma. I want to," he admitted. "But she did me dirty."

"She was just looking out for her future, baby. She was young."

"I was supposed to be in her future," he said, getting upset. "I didn't interrupt anything she had going on. I didn't ask her to change her plan or nothing. It shouldn't have been that easy for her to do that."

"Sounds like you got some things to get off your chest, son. Why don't you have that conversation so you can move on?"

"With her?" he asked.

"I didn't say that. Are you even single?" she asked. Julian laughed. "I'm asking because I really don't know."

"I'm seeing somebody," he said, smirking. "Casually."

Joyce rolled her eyes before tossing a balled up paper towel at him. "You too old to be seeing somebody casually. Get it together."

Julian laughed as he caught the paper towel. "You'll be the first to know when I get serious."

Deniece walked in the kitchen as Joyce put the potatoes in the hot oil on the stove.

"I caught up, Ma."

"Good. Cut some onions up in this while I fry this bacon. We can watch the next one after I finish."

"Momma, you watching that mess with her?"

"She has me watching it," Deniece said, laughing. Julian shook his head before laughing.

"Love and Hip Hop is like a new age soap opera for me," Joyce said. "Kept me entertained all pandemic."

"Y'all making a lot of noise," Ray said, descending the steps next to the back door.

"Time for you to wake up anyway, sleepyhead," Joyce said, smiling. Ray kissed her before greeting his children. He then walked back over to his wife.

"Finish cooking my food, woman," he teased, rubbing her back. Deniece and Julian groaned when he tapped her butt.

"Daddy!" Deniece said, holding her hand over her mouth. "We are present."

"Well get gone then," he said. Joyce giggled as he kissed her cheek.

"We were here first," Julian said, laughing.

"Technically, I was here first," Ray said. "A whole decade before y'all even came around."

"Whatever," Deniece said. "Still nasty."

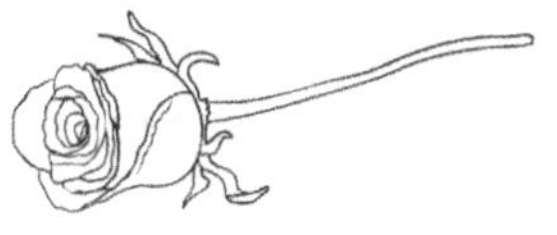

Seven | A Way Back

Tessica King smiled down at the photo album that held the entirety of her and Julian's relationship in its pages. She'd looked at it countless times since being back in her childhood room and this was the first time it didn't make her want to cry.

So many memories and shared history made Tessica question her sanity all these years. Julian was her first love and best friend. She couldn't believe that she let something as trivial as a piece of paper cause her to push him out of her life. Now here she was, divorced and trying to get him to forgive her after all these years.

It wasn't like Tessica's life had been horrible up until that point. She was okay with her decision when she made it. All of their lives, higher education had been the priority. So much so that Tessica dreamed up the perfect little life; go to college together, pledge, get married, have kids, be successful, etc. They had it all planned out and she could never figure out why Julian wanted to disrupt that. He wasn't even doing bad in school. If he didn't want to finish for himself, he could have at least finished for her.

She'd known of Brenden Washington when she first got to campus. He'd approached her a few times before she finally told him that she had a boyfriend. Surprisingly, he backed off. Tessica thought that was a quality most guys their age didn't have and respected him for it. When news got around that Julian dropped out and Tessica was single, he was the first one in her DMs. Tessica didn't waste any time filling Julian's spot.

Brenden and Tessica's relationship had been just as calculated as she and Julian's, except the history and passion wasn't there. Only the plan.

Tessica cleared her throat as the bedroom door opened and her mother walked in.

"How many times are you gonna look at these old pictures, baby?" Miss Ann said, moving a piece of Tessica's straight hair behind her ear. "I love your hair straight."

"Too much work though," Tessica said. "And I just like looking at them."

"I saw you and Julian talking at the party," she said. "Is that why you came back?"

The tone in her mother's voice made her want to roll her eyes. "No, Momma. I came back because Brenden put me out. Remember?"

"You filed for divorce honey. What did you expect?"

When Brenden was promoted to junior partner at his law firm, his hours began to increase. He began to travel more and his workload caused him so much frustration that it began to spill over into their home. He was never satisfied. Tessica couldn't do anything right in his eyes. He even began to criticize the meals she made that used to be his favorite. Her last straw was when he began to talk down on her being a housewife, which was something he wanted. Tessica hadn't even been able to use her engineering degree because they got engaged right after graduation. She was adamant about starting her career when he went to law school, but he "needed her in other ways that wouldn't allow time for that." Brenden didn't want his wife to work, but all of a sudden Tessica being a housewife didn't fit his narrative. She wasn't even upset that he wanted her to work, it was the condescending manner in which he started to bring it up.

It was as if, all of the sudden, Tessica wasn't the prize anymore. Brenden nagged about everything she did. She never had to worry about that with Julian. He loved everything about her.

"I should have stayed with Julian," she mumbled, running her hand over their high school graduation picture. He never had a problem with her ambition or any other life plan she had for that matter…

"If I can recall, you're the one who broke up with him, too," Miss Ann said, chuckling as she smoothed her baby girl's hair down in the back.

"You didn't give me much of a choice."

She frowned. "Now Tessica Marie, don't tell a lie. I never told you to break up with that boy."

"What? Mommy...you and Daddy had a fit when you found out that he dropped out." Tessica felt her face getting hot. "Remember all that, 'How will that boy support you now? What is he going to do?' You both said all that."

"Those were valid questions from your parents. We couldn't make that decision for you. We just gave you something to think about. You did that on your own so watch your tone with me. We didn't even know you broke up with him until Joyce told us."

Tessica sighed, feeling her throat tighten but she nodded in agreement. "You're right. He's still mad and I don't know how to fix it."

"Baby, do you really want to be with him?" Miss Ann said. "Or do you just not want to be alone?"

Tessica sighed, having asked herself that question before. Honestly, she hadn't even wanted to come home but she knew she wanted Julian a few months after her divorce. Once she told Brenden she wanted out of the marriage, he gave her so much time to live on his dime before cutting her off. Because she only had her degree with little to no experience, Tessica could not find a job suitable enough to support her lifestyle. She finally decided to come home in order to figure out the next steps of her life. She was sure that included Julian even if no one else did.

Miss Ann patted her daughter's thigh before hugging her. "You'll figure it out if it's meant to be."

She left her daughter alone to her memories again. Tessica began flipping through pages and came across a trip to Botanical Gardens. She laughed remembering the spur of the moment date that happened to be the same time as a school field trip.

"I'm not going in here, Ju," Tessica huffed, pulling on her braided ponytail. Julian pushed it out of her hand and she rolled her eyes. "I didn't skip school with you to end up at Botanical Gardens!"

"You didn't even want to skip school, now you're complaining about where I'm taking you?"

Tessica pushed her arms under her chest and her back into the seat, unrelenting. "Why didn't we just go to Six Flags with everyone else? It's senior ditch day."

"Because everybody there. I know you don't like lines and big crowds. Plus, I wanted you to myself," he admitted. Tessica smiled as her shoulders dropped.

"Aw, Ju," she said, running her hand over his cheek. "That's sweet."

"Right," he said. "So get out of the car and stop complaining."

Tessica rolled her eyes but unbuckled her seatbelt. She waited until Julian came around and opened the door for her before grabbing her crossbody Coach bag and hopping out of his dad's car. Looking around, Tess realized what a beautiful day it was and suddenly felt giddy about being there. She knew it would be beautiful in the sun to see all the flowers and greenery.

"Is there any special setup going on right now?" she asked as they walked hand in hand to the front door. Julian shrugged and she laughed.

"Girl, I don't know. I'm winging it."

Tessica giggled before looking at her phone to see her best friend asking where she was. She replied simply that she was on a date with her boyfriend before putting her phone back into her purse and wrapping both of her arms around one of Julian's.

"I haven't been here since middle school," she admitted. Julian nodded. Neither of them had memberships so Julian paid for their entry. While they were walking through the information center, she realized there had to be multiple classes of elementary school kids on field trips that day.

"So much for it not being crowded."

"Better than all our friends in our face all day," Julian said, Tess nodded even though she didn't mind it. Julian was never one to be in the center of attention. "Let's go to the garden maze."

For some reason, no matter the weather, it was always hotter at the zoo and at botanical gardens. It was almost as if the sun just zoomed in on the area. Tessica had a blue jean jacket on and she immediately regretted it. She remembered she had a pair of sunglasses in her bag and pulled them out.

"Take your jacket off," he said. Once she did, he threw it over his shoulder. She smiled, kissing his cheek in appreciation.

"I wish it was dark so we can see the lights," she said, walking over the stone bridge. She giggled to herself as she hopped from one stone to the next.

"Don't fall in the water, baby," he teased. Tessica turned towards him and stuck her tongue out. Out of nowhere, a little boy came running past and bumped into her. Tessica lost her balance and almost fell in but Julian grabbed her right in time.

"Ay little boy, come apologize!"

"It's okay," Tessica said, watching the group of kids turn back to them.

"Not my fault she's clumsy!" the little boy yelled back. The tribe around him began to laugh. Tessica frowned.

"Where is your teacher?"

"Minding her business like you should be."

"Aw nah," Julian said, taking off towards the kids. They began to scream and run away from him. Tessica tried to catch him but she was laughing too hard.

"Don't hurt the kids, Julian!"

"Nah, they got me messed up!" he said as he caught the ring leader. He began to tickle him and the kid burst out screaming. Tessica laughed as she made Julian put him down.

"Come on before we get put out."

Julian let Tessica pull him away. They looked at each other and laughed hard.

"If I see him again, it's on sight."

She pushed his shoulder. "Always trying to fight somebody's kid."

"That's how I'll be with ours," he said. "Can't let no kid punk me."

Tessica smiled at the mention of their future, They were still seniors in high school but it seemed they had it all figured out. They were going to the same college and Tessica expected a ring at graduation. Julian was down with the plan and often brought it up more than she did.

"Come on, love. Let's go to the butterfly house."

They walked around for a little while longer before they passed a dippin' dots stand. Of course, Tess wanted ice cream. She sat on a bench while Julian stood in line.

"Vanilla and strawberry please," she called out. Julian turned while looking at her.

"I know that."

She smiled but quickly turned around when she heard some kids coming their way. She recognized the boy who almost made her fall in the water but none of them were paying attention. Tessica smirked as she quickly stuck her foot out just before he passed. The little boy's eyes got wide as he tripped and fell over into the grass. Tessica quickly pulled her foot back and looked down at her phone as all the other kids laughed.

She looked up to see Julian walking back over with the ice cream in his hand, laughing hard.

"That's why I love you," he said, kissing her. "You're always down with the shits."

Tessica laughed before scooping the dots into her mouth. "Always."

Tessica smiled as she thought of an idea to help break Julian's ice towards her. She pulled her phone out of her back pocket and called his sister.

"Hey Niecey, I need a favor."

***

About a week later, Deniece groaned as she parked her brother's truck.

"Why didn't you just tell me we were going to Dave and Buster's instead of insisting you drive my baby?" Julian complained

"Julian shut up," Deniece said. "You always got something to say."

"You're the one who got me out of my bed on a Saturday."

"It's 4p," Deniece said. "Get over it."

"Why are we here?" He ignored her. "Are they even open?"

Deniece grunted before pushing his door open and swinging her legs out of the truck. She didn't jump down until she sent a text to Tessica letting her know that they were there. There weren't many cars in the parking lot. Deniece had confirmed that they were open now but only taking reservations. She was happy she wouldn't be going in.

"Deniece," Julian said in a warning tone. She smiled when she saw Tessica get out of her car a few feet away.

"You have a date," she said, pointing behind him. Julian frowned before turning around.

"Hey," Tessica said, softly, waiting to gauge his reaction. Julian rolled his eyes.

"I didn't agree to a date," he said, looking back at his sister.

"Well, I have your keys and I'm leaving you here. So either stay outside or go in."

Julian went to grab his keys from her and Deniece quickly moved and jumped back in the truck, locking the door. Julian pulled the handle but really got upset when she turned the ignition on.

"Deniece stop playing with me."

"Come on, Ju. Really?" Tessica said. "Just indulge me for a few hours?"

"Didn't you say you were done talking?" he snapped, turning towards her. Tessica took a step back before looking around. "What do you want?"

"I want to explain myself," she said without hesitation. "And spend time with you."

Julian sighed, looking over her soft features and full lips. He hated that he wanted to give in and she smiled, knowing that he would.

Deniece rolled the window down an inch, lifting her chin so that her lips would be closer to the crack. "Have fun now."

Julian sighed before stepping back, allowing Deniece space to drive off. Once his truck was out of the parking lot he looked at Tessica with a blank stare.

"It'll be fun," she said, biting her lip to keep from smiling so hard. "I promise."

Julian rolled his eyes. "Come on, T."

She skipped a little before clapping. Julian laughed before pulling her wrist to walk alongside her to the door. Tessica bit her lip as she looked at his side profile. Julian was always cute to her, but now he was "grown man" fine. Her heart leaped thinking of all the kisses, hugs, and intimate moments they shared even before they were fully grown. Everything she learned about how to be in a relationship came from him. She was hoping he remembered that.

"We eating here?" he asked.

"Let's play first."

Julian nodded as they walked past the restaurant part, down the corridor, and into the game room. The games chirped and sang around them as they both looked around, seeing what had changed. There were a lot of new games in the front, but Tessica could see a few they'd played years ago. Julian went over to the recharge station and asked if she had any old cards to reload. When she shook her head, he began the transaction to get new ones.

"Ju, I asked you out," she said, trying to pay for the cards. Julian pushed her hand away and she sighed.

"Pay for the food."

She smiled. "Deal." Julian smirked and she frowned. "What?"

"Nothing, I just remembered that P brought his girl here when they first started dating."

Tessica nodded in understanding. "The girl from the party? She's cute."

"Yeah, that's Sage."

"They've been together long?"

"Almost a year," Julian said. "I hooked them up."

Tessica eyed him, suspiciously. "Did you really?"

Julian laughed. "Well, I hired her and that's how they met so yeah I did."

Tessica laughed before taking one of the cards out of Julian's hand. "Come on, I want to ball."

After playing almost every game in the building, they headed back towards the front to get a table to eat.

"Now don't do too much," Tessica said. Julian frowned.

"Don't ask me out and put a limit on my food," he said. "You big money, you got it."

Tessica rolled her eyes but looked over the menu to see what she wanted. She ordered the crispy Hawaiian chicken sandwich while Julian got the beast mode bacon burger.

"Thank you for staying," Tessica said.

"What made you pick here?" he asked.

She shrugged. "I was just thinking about how much fun we used to have and thought I could remind you of that," she said, honestly. Julian nodded.

"I can admit I'm less annoyed with you right now," he said, chuckling. Tessica sighed.

"I need to know if this is worth me fighting for, Julian," she said. He ate some fries while looking at her. "I know you're still mad but it's been years and I've apologized. If you truly are done with me I need to know."

"You feel like you can make those types of ultimatums?" he asked.

"Yes," she said, nodding while she sat up straight. "I'm not asking for you to fall back in love with me today, but if you can't even forgive me then there's no point in this. Just be honest. If you feel like what I did was unforgivable, tell me. I'll leave it alone."

"It's that simple for you to leave me alone right?" he asked. Tessica frowned before she sighed, her shoulders dropping in frustration.

"I see this was a bad idea," she said. Julian chuckled.

"Why? Cause you not getting everything you want off rip? You thought I was just going to run back to you and let you do whatever you wanted. You claim you fighting for something but it sounds like you giving up real easy, little girl."

"Don't patronize me with that little girl shit," she said. "You know I don't like that."

"That's what you're acting like Tessica. How you impatient with my forgiveness? You don't get to dictate that."

"It's been years, Julian! Just tell me," she whined.

"Can I get you anything else?"

Tessica's neck snapped to look at the waitress who stepped up to the front of the booth. Julian opened his mouth but Tessica frowned.

"You see us talking right?" she snapped.

"Tessica," Julian said in a warning tone.

"Oh, I'm sorry," she said. "You two are a little loud."

"It's Dave and Buster's," Tessica said. "It's a loud place. How are we a little loud?"

Julian groaned, running his hand over his face before turning to the waitress.

"I'm sorry love," he said. "We're good."

"I'm sorry, love," Tessica mocked, turning her anger to him. "You trying to be cute? You know what, you can help me. Bring me the check so I can go! Matter of fact, here." Tessica pulled her debit card out. "Just go ahead and ring me out then bring the receipt."

She pushed the card into the waitress's hand. Rolling her eyes, the waitress walked away when Julian started laughing. Only Tessica knew it wasn't an amused laugh.

"Have you grown up at all since college?"

Tessica rolled her eyes. "She could have approached us differently."

"You think everything should move how you want it to move and that isn't realistic, love. You better be a little nicer if you even think I'm going to consider doing anything other than forgiving you."

Tessica smirked. "So, you forgive me."

"Considering how you just snapped at the waitress, I shouldn't…but I already did. I'm not mad about it anymore, but that doesn't mean I'm going to let you back into my life. You're childish as hell and I don't need this type of drama in my life. Matter of fact, I don't even want to be around you right now."

"You can't be serious," Tessica frowned. "You really mad about that?"

"You know I don't do that drama shit, Tess!" Julian said, trying not to raise his voice. Tessica just closed her mouth to make sure she didn't say anything else crazy. The waitress came back with the receipt and walked off without a word. Tessica grabbed the receipt, stuffed it in her purse while pulling her mask out. She rolled her eyes at Julian while she put it on, got up, and then walked out of the building.

"Are you going to take me home or do I need to call D?" he huffed. Tessica frowned.

"Why are you acting so upset? It wasn't that serious."

"Because you're acting like a child, Tessica," Julian said. "You haven't changed. You still a hot head who gets mad when she doesn't get her way and I don't move like that anymore. My life isn't all about making sure Tessica is happy. You gotta grow up."

"You don't have to talk to me like that," Tessica said, snatching her mask off as she walked out of the front door, stalking off towards her car. "Hurry up before I leave you!"

"I wish you would," Julian retorted, following behind her. "Now you're mad because I told you about your ass."

Tessica huffed, searching the parking lot aisle she was in to make sure she could see her car. Once it came into view, she stepped a little faster, putting more space in between her and

Julian. She heard him chuckle and she wanted to turn around and throw a rock at him.

"Just shut up, Julian!"

"I didn't say anything, Tessica," he said, imitating her voice. She couldn't help but laugh as she stood at the driver's door of her car.

"You get on my nerves."

"Obviously, I don't," he smirked as he reached for the passenger door handle. "You pulling stunts to get me alone and shit."

Tessica huffed before unlocking the door and getting in. Julian followed suit, still laughing.

"I changed my mind," she said. "Call your sister."

Julian stopped laughing, "You serious?"

"I don't want you in my car right now."

Julian ran his hand down his face before laughing in frustration. "Tessica, you something else for real."

She kept quiet as he pulled his phone out. She assumed he just sent his sister a text because he didn't make a phone call.

"I just sent you my address," he said. "Take me home and we don't have to talk ever again."

The tone in his voice made Tessica start her car, but his words hit the pit of her stomach. That wasn't what she wanted and hearing him say that confused her. They were having such a good time, she didn't know how a petty situation with a waitress turned into this.

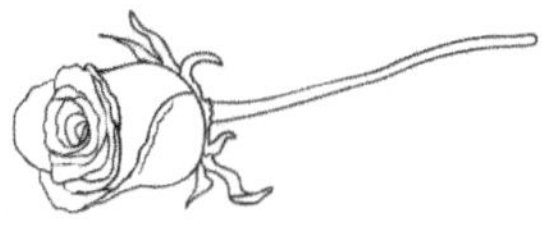

Eight | Honey to a Bee

Nicole sat in the passenger seat of her best friend's Jeep, head pounding as City Girl's blasted through the speakers. It was Sunday and they were headed to brunch at Marquee Restaurant and Lounge.

"Come on, sis!" Raina yelled. "Get hype. We haven't been outside in a whole year and some change."

Nicole fought a giggle as Raina elbowed her a few times to lighten her friend's mood.

"I'm tripping right?" Nicole asked. Raina nodded as she stopped at the light on Washington. Raina had been trying to get Nicole out of the house for the last few weeks. She'd had the previous excuse of not being vaccinated, but now that she was, Raina wouldn't take no for an answer.

The truth was that Nicole missed Julian. It had been two weeks since the water main issue and the building being closed. The most Nicole got from him was hearing his voice on zoom calls. Other than that she talked to Pierre or they corresponded through email.

She was lost as to what they were doing. One minute, they were in each other's faces every night and the next he was "too busy to return her calls or texts in a timely manner." Nicole honestly wanted to be over it, but she really liked him.

"Stop thinking about that man, we're about to see a whole lot of men," Raina said, pulling into the parking lot of the club. Nicole had been so lost in her thoughts that she hadn't even realized they were there.

Nicole nodded before pulling the visor down to check her makeup. She feathered her silk press in an attempt to add volume. She usually kept her hair in a protective style of some sort: a wig or braids. However, during quarantine she learned to take care of her natural hair and wanted to wear it more. She dyed it a copper color and wore twist-outs now. However, she preferred it pressed. The tinted moisturizer she used gave her tawny skin a natural-looking glow, especially when she smiled to show her dimples. Her long lashes curled just right to accent her makeup and light brown eyes. She glossed her full lips before blowing a kiss at herself and putting her mask on.

Raina giggled. "Girl come on before we miss our reservation."

"Don't hate," she teased.

"Cause you do too much."

"Maybe you ain't doing enough," Nicole said, rapping her favorite Kash Doll song. They both laughed while getting out of the car.

"Shut up, you know that's my song. Plus you definitely dressed down today. I told you to be fine, fine."

Nicole frowned. "I am fine, fine." She kicked her Steve Madden heel out and dusted imaginary dirt from her graphic tee. She had on a pair of destroyed jeans. The look wasn't as dressy as Raina's dress, but Nicole loved her style and always kept it cute.

"I do love those shoes."

There was no one in line so they got right in for their reservation. It was only a handful of times that Nicole had been inside Marquee when the lights were on. She thought it was crazy how things looked different in the dark when you're drunk and partying.

They were seated at a booth between the bathroom and the first bar.

"Go ahead and start those mimosas, sir!" Raina said to the waiter as they both pulled their masks off.

"No, come back!" Nicole said. "I already know what I want."

"Dang, give me a minute," Raina said. Nicole giggled before looking around. She could tell the city had been restless, it was never this many men out for brunch before the pandemic.

"I think I see one of your exes, boo," Nicole said, pointing behind her. Raina didn't even look up from the menu.

"Don't do too much," she said. "I don't have exes. Just people I used to know."

Nicole laughed before swaying in her seat to an old Jodeci song that was playing. She eyed a man walking from one of the VIP sections. He smiled at her and she politely smiled back. She inwardly rolled her eyes as he stopped on the outside of the booth, leaning over.

"What's up, beautiful, let me buy you a drink."

"Oh no thank you, it's girls' day. Maybe later."

Raina looked up from her menu as the man walked off and Nicole went back to swaying in her seat.

"Now come on now!"

"What?" Nicole looked at her innocently. "I'm not checking for no man today."

"Except Julian right?" Raina asked, raising her eyebrow. This time Nicole did roll her eyes.

"What's wrong with me wanting to be committed, Rai?"

"You're not committed, Nicole. That's what's wrong with it. That man is not claiming you. Even if he was, you're single until you're married."

"Just because I don't have a title doesn't mean we don't have a connection."

Raina huffed, sitting back to look Nicole in the eyes. "Tell me why you like this man so much. All I know is he's your boss and occasionally takes you out."

Nicole smiled, immediately feeling butterflies thinking about Julian. "I can't really explain it. We just vibe really well. He's charming and sweet even though he can be a jerk sometimes, but we have good conversation. He's ambitious and wants more for me. It's just…a feeling, I guess."

"Have y'all had sex?" Raina asked. Nicole sighed, not wanting to confirm it due to the tone in her voice.

"It's not about that, Rai. I really like him," Nicole said, biting her lip. "I feel like he could be the one. And I want to make sure he knows by my actions just how much I like him."

"You're really acting like you got a ring on your finger, Nic." Raina shook her head before sipping her drink. "You answer every time he calls don't you?"

Nicole frowned. "What's wrong with that? I want him to feel special and like I want to talk to him."

Raina chuckled. "Okay, girl."

Nicole huffed, feeling as if she was being belittled. "You know Momma and them always said you catch more flies with honey than with vinegar."

Julian was a jerk most of the time. Nicole knew that he judged her use of slang and hated how she code switched. She was sweet enough to him to get his guard down most days, but when they were out in public, Nicole could tell that he was always on alert when it came to how she moved. She hated being belittled. It wasn't always easy holding her tongue, especially when Julian corrected her.

However, her momma taught her it was easier to catch flies with honey. Julian was definitely a fly she planned to catch for the long run.

"Yeah and Momma and them also got multiple baby daddies and failed marriages," Raina snapped. "Do not use them as examples."

Not only was Raina Nicole's best friend, but they were also first cousins. Their mothers were sisters.

"I should snitch on you," Nicole teased. Raina shrugged before drinking her mimosa.

"Nothing they don't know," she said. "Why you think I never take anybody serious? My own daddy feeds me lies on a regular basis. He does it to every woman in his life. All my sibling's dads do the same thing. I don't trust any of them."

Nicole frowned. It was true that the women in their family had been through their share of heartbreak and drama. Raina's feelings were valid, but Nicole didn't want to live like that. She wanted to be open to actually holding a man accountable for what he said. She wanted to trust that the man she was with had her back and wouldn't have her outside looking stupid. She wanted true love and didn't think anything was wrong with that. No matter what Raina or anyone else in her family had to say about it.

***

As the pair walked out of Marquee, Nicole had to admit that her mood had been lifted. A day out with her best friend was exactly what she needed. Usually, a boozy brunch would have her ready to cuddle up. Although she heard what Raina said, Nicole wouldn't lie to herself about her feelings for Julian. She wouldn't mind laying up with him for the rest of the day.

As if God himself dropped a big red flag in her lap, Nicole noticed Julian's car in traffic on the way back to her place.

"I think that's him," she mumbled, squinting her eyes to make sure. Raina frowned.

"What? Your boy? What type of car he got?" Raina asked, speeding up a little. "This black F150?"

"I'm not sure if that's his…"

"Quit playing, is that him or not? That's definitely an F150? There's a woman in the car with him, Nic!"

Nicole's heart dropped a little as Raina sped up. "Don't get too close."

"My tint is dark, he doesn't know me or my car," Raina said. "We need to see who in there." Nicole gasped and put her back flat against the seat as Raina sped up and switched lanes to be closer to the truck.

"Maybe it's his sister? I've never seen her…" Nicole said. "Or a relative or something."

"Call him right now."

"Call him?" she frowned. "For what?"

"To see if he answers. He'll answer if it's a relative."

"What sense does that make?" Nicole asked. Raina sucked her teeth and repeated the command.

Nicole sighed before pulling her phone out of her clutch. She could feel the lump form in her throat as she went to her messages to get to his number. Biting her bottom lip, Nicole hit the green button and put it on speaker. Raina slowed down to stay behind the truck. Even if the phone hadn't kept ringing, Nicole could clearly see that Julian wasn't lifting a finger to answer his phone. The big screen on his console had to announce her call as his phone was always hooked to the bluetooth.

He was ignoring her.

"Call again. Call back," Raina said, gripping the steering wheel with her left hand and reaching for Nicole's phone with the other.

Nicole lifted it towards the window and out of her best friend's reach. "Watch the road."

She didn't call him back, but she did send a text message.

Hey. You busy tonight? I want to see you.

Nicole almost rolled her eyes at the message. Being sweet was disarming, but she wanted to go off. What woman was in his car that was important enough to ignore her for?

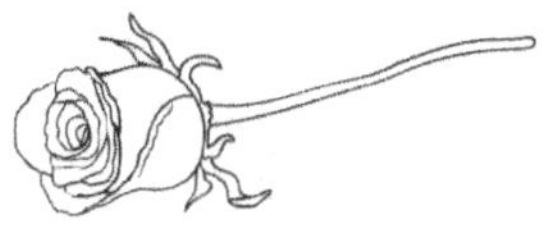

Nine | May the Best Woman Win

It was another week before Tessica decided to go to Harris Trucking & Construction and apologize. It wasn't even her idea. Although her pride was hurt, she really believed that Julian was taking things too far. Either he was going to apologize so that they could move forward or he was going to stop whatever was going on altogether.

Tessica knew Julian Harris like the back of her hand. She knew he was only being a jerk because he really wanted to forgive her. His pride was at stake, too. If he was really over Tessica like he wanted her to assume he was, he wouldn't even entertain her for a minute. That was why she was so irritated. She wasn't one to play games, but it was looking like that's what Julian wanted to do.

Her best friend was the one who convinced her to stop sulking, get cute, and take Julian lunch to apologize. Tessica found out through social media that the water break issue had been fixed and he and Pierre were back in the office.

It was a hot day in St. Louis so Tessica opted for Julian's favorite thing for her to wear; a sundress. She wore her L'agence camo silk slip dress with a pair of Gucci slides. Her curls had fallen into a wave so she brushed her edges down and left it out. While driving downtown, she made a curbside order from Seoul Taco and called Naja on the way to calm her nerves.

"Remember, go in there and be the sweet Tessica he used to drool over."

Tessica laughed, paying attention to the cars on 70 as she sped up. "Remind me how that goes again?"

Tessica met Naja in her freshman year of college. She actually had a fling with Pierre one weekend while he was visiting Julian on campus. For the next couple of weeks, she kept popping up in hopes of seeing him around. Julian thought it was funny and wouldn't tell her that Pierre didn't actually go to the school. Tessica had been the one to break the bad news to her. They became close ever since.

"Don't even know why you want him back," she teased."

"Don't do too much," Tessica said. "You should see him now, Naj. He's so grown and fine."

"I'm going to throw up," Naja said. Tessica laughed. "This is college all over again. Get off my phone. Text me how it goes."

Her thoughts ran a mile a minute while picking up the food. It wasn't until Tessica paid to park across the street that she realized she had no idea how she'd get inside the building without Julian knowing. She sighed, calling Deniece again.

"Girl, I'm tired of being the accomplice to your sneak attacks," she said, laughing.

"This the last one, I promise," Tessica said. "If he's not nice to me after this, I'll run away."

Deniece laughed. "Let me call Nicole and tell her I have someone bringing Julian lunch."

"Is that the secretary?"

"Something like that."

Tessica frowned but turned the ignition off before looking for a clean mask. "Okay, wish me luck."

"You good, boo. I'll call her now," Deniece said before hanging up. Tessica made sure there was nothing on her face before putting on her mask, grabbing the bag of food, and hurrying across the street before any cars came. She tried to open the door but realized it was locked. Looking on the side, she hit the button labeled Harris Trucking and Construction and waited.

"Harris Trucking & Construction."

"Hey it's Tessica, Deniece called about me bringing food to Julian?"

"Buzzing you in now. The elevator is on the left."

"Thank you."

Tessica smiled when she got off the elevator, seeing the woman at the desk she assumed was Nicole. Her eyes widened a little as she got off the phone.

"Hey, you can leave it here. I'll take it to him."

Tessica frowned. "I was actually hoping to eat with him."

"...Does he know you're coming?"

"It's a surprise," Tessica said. The woman smirked and Tessica felt her back straightened. She watched as the woman looked at the computer screen before looking back at her.

"He's bu…"

"Tessica King?"

Both women looked up at the sound of the voice. Tessica smiled to see Pierre coming out of an office.

"Pierre, this place is really nice. I'm proud of y'all."

"Appreciate it," he said, looking between her and Nicole. "How are you?"

"I'm good, surprising Ju with lunch," she said, holding up the bag. Pierre ran his hand down his face and chuckled.

"Let me show you where his office is."

"He's on a conference call," the secretary blurted out. Pierre stopped and looked at her.

"I know, I was on it, too," he said, before looking back at Tessica. "Come on."

Tessica followed Pierre around the hall and sighed. "I'm sure he told you about last week."

"He did," Pierre said. "But that's not my business."

"Is he really mad?"

"You know Julian, he brushed it off but don't expect a warm welcome."

"That's why I brought the food," she said. They laughed.

"Don't forget this is a place of business," he said, pointing to the door. Tessica playfully rolled her eyes.

"I won't."

Tessica waited until Pierre went back in the direction of his office before she took her mask off and knocked on the door.

"Come in."

Tessica held the bag up in front of her face as she slid inside and closed the door behind her. She could hear other voices coming from his computer so she peaked around the bag and smiled. Julian rolled his eyes but didn't hide his smile. Tessica took that as an invitation and began to quietly take the food out of the bag and place them on the end table by his love seat. She looked around in awe. It was simply decorated, but it gave Tessica an opportunity to get to know the grown-up Julian a little.

He had pictures of his parents and a few family pictures of the Harris clan. There was a dark blue accent wall behind Julian but the rest of them were an off-white color. The accent wall had wooden shelves that were connected by bar connectors. The shelves were the same wood that was used to make his desk. There was no carpet but his desk and the love seat had neutral colored area rugs. Tessica sat down as he ended his call. She waited for him to speak, but he didn't. He just looked at her.

She exhaled before holding up a plastic fork. "Peace offering."

"You lucky I'm hungry."

Tessica smiled as he got up and came to sit down. He looked over the burrito and Gogi & waffles and nodded in approval. She was proud that she remembered one of his favorite meals from there.

"I'm waiting for my apology."

She sighed. "I'm sorry I got all extra. That wasn't cute but I did mean it when I asked what you wanted to do. If you don't want to forgive me, Ju, I get it, but just let me know if I'm wasting my time."

They fell into a comfortable silence while eating. Tessica realized Julian was thinking about what she said because of how focused he was on the food and how slow he chewed. She enjoyed her food and her view. Where her high school sweetheart Julian had braids and braces, this one was more refined with flawless waves and an amazing smile. The small cut near his eyebrow was still visible but not as prominent as it used to be. He was still slim, but evidence of his time in the gym was clear. Tessica never imagined him with a beard, but now all she wanted to do was pull it while they kissed.

"You're not fighting for nothing," he suddenly said. Tessica smiled before scooting next to him. He stopped her and she frowned. "But I need some time to figure out where my head is and see how serious you are."

Tessica nodded. "I get it. I didn't expect you to just fall back in love with me. I just need to know I have a chance."

Julian looked at her and nodded. Before he could say anything else, his office door opened. Tessica frowned to see Nicole, the secretary standing there.

"Your appointment tomorrow got rescheduled," she said before looking between the two.

"Did you change it on my schedule?" Julian asked. She nodded but since he was looking down at his food, he hadn't seen it. Nicole looked at Tessica and her nose flared. Tessica immediately recognized the look of jealousy and smirked, sitting back against the loveseat. "Nicole?"

"Yes, I did," she said, still looking at Tessica. "I thought you were taking a late lunch today?"

"She surprised me," Julian said, finally looking up. "Thanks though."

Nicole sighed before walking back out of the door, leaving it slightly open.

"She seems a bit friendly," Tessica said, trying to choose her words. "For a secretary."

"She actually runs the office," Julian said, finishing his food "This was good as hell. Now Momma gonna be mad I'll be too full for dinner."

"I'm sure you'll be hungry by then," Tessica said. "Tell your mom I said hi. She looked so good at their party."

"She asked about you."

"She did? What she say?"

"None of your business," he said, throwing a rolled up paper towel at her, Tessica rolled her eyes.

"So why you even tell me?"

"Cause I can."

Tessica gave him a dead stare and he just laughed. "I have to get back to work. Thanks for lunch."

Tessica nodded, feeling better about her plan to surprise him She stood up and held both her arms out. Julian looked her up and down before laughing and pulling her into a hug,

"Call me later?" she asked, inhaling his scent."

"I will," he said. She smiled. "Let me walk you out."

"No, I got it," she said, grabbing her purse. "You get back to work."

Julian chuckled as Tessica walked away, giving him a view of what he'd get once he stopped being fake mad.

***

"You've been avoiding me. Who got you too busy for me?"

Julian sighed as he looked at Nicole's pouting lips on his phone. Ever since Tessica's pop up last week at work, he had been avoiding her. He hadn't even been in the office much with the excuse that he didn't feel too well. Pierre made him take a covid test and although it came back negative, Julian decided to stay out the rest of the week.

Nicole's text had gone unanswered so Julian wasn't shocked that she was calling to fuss. However, she didn't have to look so fine doing it. He was sure she made sure she was oozing sex appeal before calling him and he wasn't mad at it. Her hair was darker than she usually wore it and stopped at her shoulders. It was full and wavy and covered some of her face but her glossed lips were in perfect view. He thought she didn't have a shirt on the way she was laid across her bed, but he saw she had on one of those sleeveless dresses she liked to wear around the house when she adjusted herself.

"Why you look so good right now?" he asked, licking his lips.

"I look like this all the time," she giggled. "You'd know if you spent time with me outside of work."

Julian's eyes scanned as much of her body as he could see before looking back into her eyes. "Is that an invitation?" He watched her exhale before she bit her lip and nodded. Biting his own, he nodded as well before sitting up on the couch. "You want anything on the way?"

Nicole shook her head. "I just want you."

Julian grinned before telling her that he was on the way. She whined and told him not to hang up. "Now you acting up."

"I miss you," she said, rolling over so she was on her back, now holding the phone up. Julian frowned at the angle doing more than what she was already doing.

"Damn Nic, I get it," he teased. She laughed before sitting up.

"Good, put some pep in your step then," she said, sticking her tongue out.

"Did you cook?" he asked, looking around for his sneakers.

She sighed. "Not today. I didn't feel like it." He just looked at her. "Stop it. I'll cook breakfast."

"You talking big today," he said, catching the innuendo. "Better back it up."

"I got you."

Although Julian could see the lust in her eyes, he wasn't sure what she was on. The last time they'd gotten close to having sex, she'd changed her mind. Julian wasn't pressed about it, he didn't mind spending time with Nicole. He did actually like her, but he didn't want to play games either. So, he knew he'd be patient and wait until she made an actual move to take things further when he got there.

Nicole had other plans.

Julian stumbled back a little but their lips never lost a beat, both of them groaning in satisfaction after the shock of Nicole pushing him up against her door wore off. She pulled his unbuttoned jacket from his body, needing to be as close to him as possible. Julian's hands went from both of her cheeks to gripping her hips. The smack that sounded when he ended their kiss was loud in the quiet of her living room but the moan that came from Nicole as he bit at the right side of her neck filled it quickly. Nicole walked backward, pulling him with her all the way to her bedroom. Julian gripped at the dress, pulling it up as he kissed her.

"You better stop me now," Julian groaned as he kissed along her collar bone. Nicole sat up a little and pulled the dress all the way off. Julian's tongue immediately went to work as her legs opened wider to move him closer. "Love, how is it possible that your skin is so soft?" he asked. Nicole didn't have time to tell him she'd been using a new body wash.

"Julian," she moaned. "Babyyyy."

"I'm right here," he groaned against her belly. "I'm here, love." He pulled a condom out of his wallet and placed it on the bed next to her before standing up. Nicole sighed heavily as she watched him take his sneakers and sweats off. Once he was out of them, she stood up and kissed him hard. She squealed a little in his mouth when he palmed her backside and picked her up. Sitting down on the edge of her bed, Julian ran his hands up her bare back while they kissed. Nicole pressed her middle to his and he groaned. His hands shook a little as he rubbed her thighs. Her kisses were becoming erratic and hungry.

"Julian," she said, impatiently.

"Let me enjoy this," he whispered. Nicole huffed a little but inhaled sharply as his hand wrapped around her waist and pressed against her center from behind. "You hear me?"

"Yes, baby," she said, dropping her head to his shoulder as he stroked the ache inside of her.

"You gonna let me take my time?" he asked, kissing her shoulder. She moaned before nodding. "I'm gonna make sure you enjoy this," he said, making her look at him as she began to rotate her hips on his hand. He slid his lips over her nipple before letting his tongue taste it again.

"You want to cum for me?"

"It feels so good already baby," Nicole cried. Julian's erection pushed against his boxers. He made her stand up before commanding her to lay back at the head of her bed. She quickly did as she was told while he took his boxers off. Nicole spread her legs as he lay on top of her. She sighed in contentment from his body weight pressing against her. She leaned up to kiss him sweetly before pushing her head back into her pillow as two of his fingers entered her smoothly. Her mouth fell open as he kissed her chin.

"Rock your hips like you were on my lap," he instructed. As soon as Nicole did it her eyes widened.

"Ahh, ooh shit."

Julian gave her a cocky smile. "Yeah, talk to me, baby."

She bit her lip as her leg began to shake. "Julian put the condom on."

He chuckled before kissing her. "Not until you cum once."

"Julian!" She whined.

"Just do what I said," he demanded. "You right there," he said, twisting his fingers. "I feel it."

"I don't, I can't," Nicole said. She couldn't find the words to tell him that she never had an orgasm and wasn't sure what she was supposed to be feeling. He looked at her before kissing her deeply.

"Look at me, love," Julian whispered against her lips. Her stomach dropped when she looked into his eyes and she moaned loudly. "Just feel it."

Nicole closed her eyes and exploded. She stopped moving and tried to catch her breath. He wasn't her first sexual experience, but that was the most pleasure she'd ever gotten and they hadn't even had sex yet. She needed a moment to regroup, but she heard the condom wrapper open and a few moments later Julian was raising her left leg up.

"That face you made was sexy," he said, sliding into her. Nicole gripped his shoulders. "Let's see if I can make it again."

***

Although Julian spent the weekend with Nicole, he found himself right back in Tessica's face a few days later. They were at his place, reminiscing on old times and discussing their music preferences back then. Tessica hooked her phone up to the sound bar under his mounted television, going through different songs to see if Julian would remember them or not.

"Oh snap!" she said, tapping her finger on the phone before standing up. "This the one right here!"

Julian grinned, watching Tessica jump up with her hands in the air as the base dropped.

"Say what yo name is? Oh yeah, that fits ya girl!" she sang along with Chris Brown as she imitated his earlier dance moves. Julian laughed as he pushed his back into the couch and continued to watch her. "You know this was our jam when it first came out! You thought you were Chri…"

"No, I didn't," he lied.

Tessica grinned before turning to him and grinding her pelvis in the air, her back was straight and her arms were curved at her side. Julian laughed, knowing that she was imitating him.

"On and poppin!" she said, her voice different this time. She laughed as Julian leaned up, pulling her back on the couch.

"Stop playing with me," he said, dragging her next to him. She giggled as she danced a little, snapping her fingers to the beat.

"This first album was the best."

"Now all his stuff sounds the same," Julian said. Tessica nodded in agreement. He looked around for her remote as she got comfortable at his side. "Want to watch a movie?"

Tessica frowned. "I want to go out. I'm hungry."

"You always want to go out," he said. Tessica looked up at him with a raised eyebrow.

"Did you eat yet?"

"No, but we can order food and chill."

Tessica pouted, but once she realized Julian wasn't trying to move, her shoulders dropped.

"Fine, but I want Broadway Oyster Bar."

His mind immediately went to Nicole but he tried to shake it off. He failed because her loud laugh popped up in his mind. She was loud for no reason sometimes, but Julian would only admit to himself that he liked it.

"Hey," Tessica said, touching his hand. "You okay?"

"Yeah…go ahead and order the food. I'll go get it after I use the bathroom."

"Okay."

"I want…"

"I know what you want," she said, smiling. Julian leaned over and kissed her forehead before getting up. He saw her blush out of the corner of his eye and he chuckled while walking away.

He went to the bathroom attached to his bedroom to get his thoughts together. He couldn't be thinking about Nicole while chilling with Tessica.

"Maybe I need a break from both of them," he mumbled after throwing water on his face. He wasn't sure how he ended up in this dilemma when just a few months ago, he wasn't even trying to seriously date anyone. He was just having fun with Nicole. They had a good vibe, but he knew she wanted more. Tessica showing up and applying pressure was the last thing he thought would have put him in this mindset. Not wanting to make the wrong decision, Julian thought about just cutting both of them off.

Tessica decided to ride with Julian to get the food. They began reminiscing about their younger years and Julian had to admit it was nice. Some of the moments he forgot or would be sure that she did, Tessica recalled vividly. He sighed, realizing that she was indeed genuinely trying to get back in his good graces. The revelation allowed a small fracture to the wall he'd built up to keep her out.

When they got back to Julian's, Tessica sat on the marble island while Julian sat on his stool and ate dinner.

"Why are you up there?" he asked. Tessica shrugged and smiled.

"I like feeling taller than you," she said, giggling. Julian looked up at her and smirked.

"Yeah okay. I'll still beat you up," he teased.

Tessica sighed. “I know you still got questions.”

Julian looked down at his food. “You being a brat about answering them though.”

“I’ll answer them now.”

Julian didn’t respond but got up to throw their empty containers away. Tessica turned to where her legs were dangling off the counter to watch him move around the kitchen. She sat quietly but tapped her nails against the marble every few seconds. She gasped when Julian turned and walked into her space, pushing her knees apart to stand between her legs.

“Are we going to talk?”

“You can’t get mad at what I ask,” he stated, his hands sliding up her sides and the outline of her breast.

Tessica gasped. “But can I get a kiss first?” Julian smirked at how her question came out as a whisper.

“You don’t get any kisses unless you agree,” he said. Tessica huffed before stretching her legs around his waist and locking her feet together.

“That's rude.”

“I can control myself as long as I’m not kissing you,” he admitted. Tessica tightened the muscles in her legs to bring him closer then pecked his lips.

“What if I don’t want you to control yourself?

“Tell me what I want to hear,” Julian said, pulling her closer to the edge. Tessica pushed against him and moaned. “I don't want you answering any questions right now because you’d say just about anything,” he said.

“I’m in my right mind,” Tessica said, closing her eyes as he rubbed his nose against her neck.

“So agree then.”

“I agree, Julian.” She opened her eyes to see Julian’s slanted and staring at her lips. His were slightly open as a light breath escaped them, warming hers before she pushed theirs together.

Julian's hands massaged her back as they kissed and Tessica was sure her head was going to pop off from the pressure. She whined and wiggled in her seat on the counter as he pulled away from her. Julian laughed.

"Why are you playing with me?" She whined. He bit her bottom lip and pulled back.

"Stop whining, we gotta talk right?"

Tessica sighed but nodded.

Ten | A Right Now Vibe

"Nicole knows about Tessica," Julian said to Pierre before taking a swig of his beer.

Julian, who was busy moving around his kitchen, stopped at the counter and looked at his cousin.

"You told her?" he asked. Julian shook his head.

"She put two and two together after Tess came to the office the other day."

"I figured that would happen," Pierre admitted. "She was sizing her up when I came out of the office."

Julian sighed. "That definitely was some info you could have shared, bro."

"What she say?"

"Nothing for real."

"So how you know that she knows."

"I told you how she came in the office?" Julian asked. Pierre shook his head. Julian finished his beer while telling his cousin about the awkward interaction. "Since then she's been making slick comments. You know how women are. 'Who got you so busy that you're avoiding me. You must have been talking to your other girlfriend.' or something like that." Pierre laughed before going back to preparing his food. "It's not funny."

"What's not funny?"

Julian turned to see Sage walking down the hallway. It wasn't until she reached for her half-empty wine glass that Julian even noticed it in front of him. She sat on the stool next to him at the island and winked at Pierre.

"His woman problems."

"I don't have a woman so I don't have woman problems."

Sage eyed him, amused. "Um hum. I heard you been doing a juggling act. You should be tired."

Julian smiled before rubbing his beard. "Not tired enough. Sage, when are you going to put me on Carmen? She's taking this friend thing too far."

Pierre frowned as his woman giggled before sipping her wine. "Carmen does not want you. Besides, even if she did, I refuse to lead my friend into your circus."

"She doesn't know what she wants."

Sage laughed but Pierre sucked his teeth. "What did you come over here for?"

Julian threw both of his hands up in the air. "I can't come visit my cousin? So much for brotherly love."

"Besides sounding stupid, I told you I had plans tonight," Pierre said, eyeballing Sage as she swayed in her chair to the jazz music playing. Julian rolled his eyes.

"Y'all act like an old married couple, nobody wants to be bored to death anyway."

Pierre gave his cousin a dead stare but Sage smiled. "Goodnight, Julian."

Julian rolled his eyes before picking his phone up from the marble countertop. For a moment he wanted to call Tessica but hadn't really talked with her since they finally had that talk. Although she answered his questions and Julian got out everything he wanted to say, he still wasn't all too happy and willing to take her back. Instead, he pulled up Nicole's contact as he exited his cousin's apartment.

She answered on the fourth ring.

"Took you long enough."

"Excuse me?"

"To answer the phone...what's up? Can I come chill with you?"

Nicole snickered. "I'm actually not available tonight."

Julian frowned. "Oh, you busy? My bad what you got going on?"

"I'm not busy," she said. "Just not available to you tonight."

Julian shut his car door and waited for his Bluetooth to connect. "You're dramatic. All you had to say is no."

"And all you have to do is answer the phone when I called you earlier. So here we are."

Julian's nose scrunched. "What are you even mad about?"

"You make time for what you want to make time for," Nicole mumbled, thinking of the woman who came to the office to see him and the woman who she saw in his truck. She didn't even know if they were even the same person. Julian could be seeing multiple people. That made her cringe.

"I'm trying to make time for you." Julian ran his hand down his face, exhaling as he focused on the road ahead of him.

"Julian, you're inconsistent as hell and expect me to drop everything so you can come chill."

"I talk to you every day, Nicole."

"At work."

"...We still talk every day."

Nicole groaned. "Bye Julian."

Julian softened his tone. "Why you acting like that? You don't want to see me?" Nicole sighed, but didn't hang up. "I want to see you."

"Do you really?" she asked. Julian smiled because of the noticeable difference in her tone.

"You know I like chilling with you."

"You don't act like it," she whined.

"I'm trying to come see you right now, but you playing. Who don't want to see who?"

After a long silence, Nicole sighed. "Hurry up before I change my mind."

On the way to her house, Julian wondered why Nicole was switching up on him. It was true that he had been spending more time with Tessica and less with her, but he was sure she didn't know that. Nicole never pressed him about when they weren't together, so he wasn't sure what her issue was now.

Julian prayed that Nicole wasn't trying to argue while he walked to her front door. He had enough to deal with at work on a daily basis, he didn't feel like hearing anything negative. He sent her a text to let her know he was outside before ringing the doorbell. She answered the door a few moments later.

Julian was shocked to see her natural hair out and wild, but he liked it. He smiled at her, taking her temperature before stepping up into the threshold of the door. Nicole looked him up and down before she blushed and moved to let him in.

"I like your hair," he said, gently pulling a strand of it after she locked the door. Nicole's eyes widened as she pulled her hair back with her hands as if she was making a ponytail before letting it go.

"Thanks, I just took it down. I get it done tomorrow."

"You should wear it natural," he said. Nicole shrugged, moving around him to walk into her living room.

"It's too much work." He watched as she plopped down on her couch, different hair products spread out on her coffee table as a Pandora station played on her wall-mounted television. "What were you out doing?"

"At P's," he said, sitting on the couch next to her after taking off his shoes at the door. "They boring."

"So you hit me up, huh?" she asked, smirking. "I'm just as boring."

"I like being boring with you," he said, tapping her thigh. Nicole just smiled before she began closing up containers and stacking them on top of each other.

"Give me a second."

Julian nodded as she got up and cleaned the table off, taking everything to the back. A few minutes later she came back with her hair up in a bun. Julian frowned at the fact that she'd put a long matching cardigan over the lounge set she had on. He chuckled when she sat on the opposite side of the couch.

"Come here," he demanded. "Stop playing with me."

"I'm not playing with you, Julian," she said, softly. He just looked at her until she stood up, moving to sit next to him. When she was within reach, he pulled her onto his lap and hugged her waist. Nicole groaned in protest as he kissed all over the side of her face.

"Why you acting like you don't want me here with you?" he whispered against her neck. Nicole sighed. "You didn't miss me?"

He kept feathering her face with kisses, rubbing her side until her shoulders relaxed and she leaned more into him. Julian wrapped her tighter in his arms until she turned her face to his and quickly kissed his lips. Julian returned the affection before pulling back to look at her.

"What's up?" he asked. Nicole shook her head before laying her head on his shoulder.

"How was your day?"

"I told you it was boring," he said, laughing. "Did you cook?"

She nodded. "You want me to fix you a plate?" He nodded. "Do you even care what it is?"

"Everything you cook is good," he said. Nicole laughed before getting up.

"Yeah okay."

Julian relaxed as she fixed his plate, satisfied that it didn't take him long to remove her attitude. That's what he liked about Nicole. All she really wanted was his attention and only acted up when she didn't get it.

He noticed the Pandora station was set to some artist he wasn't familiar with. Julian rolled his eyes before changing it to the 90's R&B station. Nicole brought his plate in and he rubbed his hands together watching the steam roll off the plate. It was baked chicken with some type of gravy, mashed potatoes, and asparagus. She put it down in front of him with a Corona.

"Thanks, mama," he said, slapping her butt in appreciation. Nicole smirked but walked around the table to sit back in her original spot on the couch.

"Let me know if you need anything else."

"You got me together," he said. Nicole bit her lip to stop blushing.

"I can't stand you," she said. "Always smooth talking."

"You like it," he said before digging into his plate.

"If only you were consistent," she mumbled.

Julian chuckled. "I can leave if you gonna be throwing shots all night."

"So I can't voice my feelings?"

"Is that what you're doing? Cause I haven't heard a feeling yet. Put your big girl panties on and say what you mean."

She sighed, biting her lip while looking around the room. Julian could see her eyes get glossy, but she shook her head before clearing her throat. When she didn't say anything, he went back to eating his food. The uncomfortable silence made him decide to leave once he was done eating. Instead of letting her clear the table, he took it into the kitchen and rinsed it off in the sink. Throwing his empty Corona bottle away, Julian went back into the living room to grab his keys off the table.

"Come lock the door," he said. Nicole sighed before getting up to stop him.

"Julian, I just want some assurance that you aren't just playing with me," she said, grabbing his hand. "Is that too much to ask?"

"Have you asked it before?" he frowned, looking at her. "And I never played with you."

"I know you're dating other people," Nicole said. "That's playing."

"I ever tell you I wasn't?" he asked. Nicole frowned.

"Well, leave me alone then!"

"Is that what you want?" he asked.

She frowned even more before whining and stomping her foot. "No, Julian. I want you to commit to me."

Julian shook his head, trying not to laugh. "You cute as hell when you whining."

"I'm not playing with you right now," she said, crossing her arms. Julian sighed before pulling her into him. She struggled a little but he held her tight.

"Chill out," he said against her chin before kissing her a few times. "Why you doing all that?"

"Julian," she whined.

"I'm here with you right now right?" he asked. Nicole stayed silent as he kissed up her neck. Julian inhaled her scent before running his tongue across her flesh. When he felt her uncross her arms, he grabbed the back of her neck and kissed her. "I'm here," he said in between kisses. "Okay?"

Nicole nodded as Julian began to walk her backward towards her bedroom.

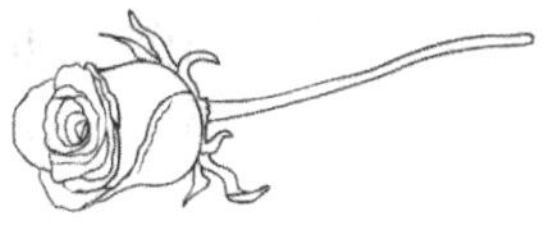

Eleven | The Last One Left

Julian thought he would be happy to be back outside, but he was starting to get burned out on events. He wondered why he had to be in attendance for Sage's 29th birthday dinner, but Pierre insisted. It was in a private dining area of Prime 1000. Julian had visited the restaurant before and hadn't even noticed there was a downstairs. He didn't think Sage had this many friends to fill a room.

"Happy birthday, mean girl," Julian said, handing Sage a wrapped bottle of her favorite wine. She hit his arm but took the bottle.

"Thanks, jerk. I'm surprised you don't have a date."

Julian smirked. "Chill out." He looked around the room and found an empty seat next to Alondra, Sage's sister, who was on the other side of Carmen. He nodded before going to sit down. "Hello, ladies."

"Switch me seats," Alondra said. "My man is on the way."

"Oh, she got a man," he teased, getting up. Alondra laughed before she scooted to the next seat, moving her purse in the empty seat next to her. "That was your plan all along huh?" he said, smiling at Carmen.

She snickered and shook her head. "Hey friend."

"You look nice."

Carmen's smile reached her eyes as she did a little dance and placed her hands on top of her breasts. "Why thank you. I do what I can." They both laughed.

The room was dimly lit with soft yellow light all around the room. The table they were at was long with a few floral centerpieces and votive candles in tall vases. Besides them, there were a few other people he didn't recognize and his aunt and uncle. He frowned, having just seen them, before getting up to greet them properly.

"Hey Auntie," he said, kissing her cheek. "What's up, Unc? I got y'all outside?"

"Hey nephew," Jaren said. "He thinks everything for Sage is a big deal," he teased. "Lovesick."

"Leave my baby alone," Janet said. "At least she's a good girl."

Julian nodded, deciding not to joke about Sage as he usually did seeing as it was her birthday. He made small talk with them a little longer before Sage and Pierre walked in. Everyone stood up and clapped, wishing her a happy birthday right from the door. Julian went back to his seat next to Carmen.

"You must have picked her outfit out," he said. Carmen laughed.

"I did," she admitted.

"I can tell, you did good."

Carmen smiled. Sage was modest most of the time, so when Julian saw her outfit, he knew her best friend had something to do with it. It wasn't too revealing, it just wasn't Sage's style. It was a black sequin two-piece set with a long skirt, a split coming up to her thigh. The top tied under her breasts and revealed a little of her stomach. Julian couldn't see her shoes from where he sat, but he was sure they were heels because Sage was not up to Pierre's chin on a regular day.

"I refuse to cry," Sage said. "Thank y'all for coming out. I know it's been a crazy year, but I appreciate everybody here, especially my baby for putting this together," she said, running her hand over Pierre's cheek. "You make me feel so special."

Everyone awed as Pierre took Sage's hand from his face and kissed it before escorting her to her seat.

"So where's your date?" Carmen asked. Julian chuckled.

"Date?"

"I know you have a team somewhere."

"You want to be on it?" Julian teased. Carmen rose an eyebrow.

"Don't do too much."

Julian laughed. "If you want me, Carmen, just say that."

She rolled her eyes before turning towards Sage. The waitress stopped behind Julian to take his order while everyone else began to talk amongst themselves. He did wonder why he hadn't brought a date. Pierre asked him if he wanted a plus one and Julian immediately said no. He had to be honest with himself to admit that he still had feelings for Tessica. He thought it was cute how she was trying so hard to get him back. At first, he just wanted to see how far she was willing to go but now he was torn with his own intentions. All of his old feelings for her were coming back but two things were stopping him.

He didn't fully trust her yet. He was content with believing she truly regretted what she did, but he had no trust that she wouldn't do it again. Yes, him and Pierre's business was successful, but it was still technically new. God forbid something happened. Would Tessica up and leave again?

Nicole had proven herself loyal to Julian even without a commitment. Julian knew that Nicole would ride out whatever with him, but there were a lot of things she did that he found annoying. Could he overlook that and his past with Tessica and choose Nicole?

His cousin's voice brought him out of his thoughts.

"You want your gifts now?" he asked.

"Yes, please," Sage said, sweetly. Julian thought it was so funny how her feminine energy automatically responded to Pierre.

"Alright," Pierre said with a proud smile. "This first one is just something light."

"Light my ass," Julian said, seeing the Chanel bag. Everyone laughed as Sage squealed.

"P! You got it? You really listen to me, baby?" she cried before pulling the box out of the bag. "Oh, it's wrapped so pretty I don't want to disturb it."

"Girl!" Alondra said. "Open that up now, I want to see."

"It's the one I've wanted that I showed you months ago," Sage said, confidently, as she untied the bow. "I already know."

Pierre just smiled as Sage squealed again once the small green bag was in her hands. She slid it on her arm before kissing him repeatedly.

"I got something else," he said. Sage went back to looking at the purse, trying to carefully put it back in the box.

"What."

Everyone gasped as Sage turned back to Pierre to see him out of his chair and on one knee. He licked his lips as his left elbow rested on his knee with the box in his hand. Everyone began to cheer as Sage became fixated on the box. She ran her nail over the top of it before looking at Pierre with tears in her eyes.

"First of all, I gotta thank my cousin for forcing me to hire you last year."

"Name the first kid Julian and we all good," Julian yelled. Everyone laughed.

"I was annoyed by everything you did but I quickly realized it was because I wanted you in my life. It wasn't long after that I realized I needed you in my life and soon after that, when you stopped being stubborn, I realized you are my life. Some people might think this is too soon but I was raised to realize when something is worth it, you secure it."

"I know that's right, son."

"That's my boy!"

Sage giggled through her tears. "You sound like a smart man.

"We'll see how smart you are when you answer this question," Pierre said before opening the box. "Sage, will you marry me?"

"Of course, I will," she said, leaning over to kiss him. Everyone cheered before Pierre put the ring on her finger. Sage leaped into his arms, making them fall over onto the floor. Everyone laughed and recorded them. After a few more moments, Carmen and Alondra ran over to Sage screaming to see the ring. Julian laughed as Pierre walked over to him and his parents.

"Good job, son," Jaren said.

"I'm so happy one of you is settling down," Janet said, eyeing her nephew.

"See what you did?" Julian asked. Pierre laughed. "Congrats P, I'm happy for you. Sage isn't that annoying."

"You always playing," Pierre said, laughing.

***

It was going on ten in the morning and Nicole wasn't at work. Julian wouldn't even be so pressed except they had a meeting to prepare for and Pierre was irritating.

"Call her again," Pierre said. "I'll set up for the meeting but make sure she's okay. Maybe something happened. Maybe she has Covid."

Julian sighed, waving his cousin off. "I printed the reports so just go get them. I'll make some coffee."

Pierre nodded before heading off to the conference room. They had two important meetings today. Pierre was working on a dedicated run for 5 drivers and Julian was working on a government contract for some construction that was projected to last at least 3 years. Both contracts would secure a lot of money for the Harris boys.

Nicole knew that both of these meetings were important. She better have been sick or dying to be this late. The show had to go on, but Julian did want to make sure she was at least okay. He decided to send a text, hoping she would at least respond, before checking her social media accounts. The elevator dinged and he looked up in disbelief to see her walking through it. She had a frown on her face when she took her mask off but nothing looked physically wrong with her.

"Something happened?" he asked. Nicole frowned, looking up from her desk as she put her purse on it.

"No."

"You're not dying?"

She huffed. "No, Julian."

"So you just show up two hours late, not answering our calls and think shit cute?"

"It's not that serious."

"We have important meetings today, Nicole! Please don't start this ratchet shit."

She chuckled. "That's what you think of me anyway, so why not?"

He frowned. "What?"

"Look, the meetings don't start for another 20 minutes. I'm here. Stop making it a big deal."

"You acting like this 'cause you assume I'm messing with other women?"

Nicole turned and looked at him. "Why would I be mad about that? We just kicking it right?"

Julian groaned, running his hand down his face. "All this shit outside of work doesn't even matter right now. I'm your boss so act like you got some sense. You know you can't just walk in nobody's place of business two hours late without a reason. So please don't play me for a lame right now, Nicole. You know better."

Nicole stood her ground, arms folded under her breast with her back straight. “Don’t be an asshole.”

“Don’t be passive aggressive,” Julian squared up with her. Nicole’s confidence faltered as she bit her lip. “You know I don’t like that indirect attitude. If you have something to say then say it so I can go back to work.”

Nicole dropped her arms down to her side. “I’m done going back and forth with you, Julian. I’ve told you I’m not in the business of casual dating.”

“But that’s what we’ve been doing,” Julian thought. “I heard you the first time you said it.”

“So why are you still on my line?” Nicole asked with conviction. Julian chuckled.

“You still answer it,” he said, looking down the hallway. He was over this conversation.

“You’re treating me like an option, Julian. I don’t like it.”

Julian frowned. “That’s what you are. Nicole, I never promised you anything.”

She laughed, but Julian could tell it was not out of amusement. “You men kill me. You talk nice, spend time, lay up whenever you want, get jealous if we even mention dating other men. But when it comes down to the responsibility of actually being committed, you think your word overpowers your actions.”

“We agree..”

“No,” she cut him off. “You agreed to keep it casual between us but you knew I liked you beyond that. If you had no intentions of taking it further, Julian, you should have left me alone! It’s not always on the woman to heed signs. You can take some accountability for that at least, damn!”

Julian sighed. “...You’re right,” he admitted. “I knew this wasn’t casual for you.” He wouldn’t lie and say that seeing her eyes become glossy didn’t hit him in the chest. He wasn’t a bad guy. He had always been upfront with Nicole. He was courteous after sex with her, they had nice conversation and he did care fo her on some level. Was it really his fault that she read more int that than he could give her at the moment?

“And it wasn’t just casual for you either at some point,” sh pointed out. Julian didn’t protest. “I felt us getting closer. Wha changed, Julian?”

Tessica is what changed. He thought. “Nicole...I can’t really d this right now. We have a lot going on this week, you know that.”

Nicole sighed, putting her hand up as she clutched her purse i her other hand. “Yep. I knew all that. This conversation is done but just so you know, Pierre will be coming to speak with yo about the resignation I put in. Since I’m not the ratchet, no clas having woman that you think I am, I gave a two-week notice. Bu to be clear...I don’t want to talk to you again. You can email me i it’s something other than my normal duties that you need.”

“You’re being childish...you know I…”

“Well, fire me then,” she said, cutting him off again. Julian jus looked at her. Nicole smirked before turning to walk out of hi office door. “Goodbye.”

Twelve | Let the Chips Fall

Sage exhaled as Pierre guided her onto the elevator of the office building early that morning. They had an amazing night and although she wasn't thrilled with her new part-time job, she was happy to help her man in need. Getting to spend more time with him was a plus.

Sage was a whole fiancé. She still couldn't believe it. From last year, arguing with Pierre in his conference room to now, they'd come full circle. What a difference a year made.

"Baby, pay attention."

Sage giggled as Pierre held the empty desk chair out for her.

"Can I make coffee first?" She smirked. "Aren't I the assistant now?"

"Office manager," he corrected. "You're nobody's assistant."

Sage bit her lip. "You're making it hard for me to pay attention, handsome."

Pierre smiled before patting the chair. Sage strutted around the desk before putting her purse down. She yelped when Pierre's heavy hand came down against her butt.

"Reset the passwords with those instructions," he said, pointing to a notepad. "I'll start the coffee."

Sage sighed and nodded, hitting the power button on the Mac and rolling further under the desk. She said a quick prayer that she wouldn't mess anything up.

Once Pierre told her about Nicole leaving, she insisted that she help out until they found a replacement. Sage was in between clients at the moment with her consulting business so she needed something to fill her time. He promised to show her the ropes for a few days before turning over the reins.

The aroma of the Dunkin' Donuts Caramel coffee hit her nose before her fiance rounded the corner. He laughed as Sage did a wiggle in the chair, holding both of her arms up to grasp the mug meant for her.

"I put a little almond milk in it so it should be cool enough to drink."

"Where has this man been all my life?" Sage thought. *"He even remembers how I like my coffee."*

Pierre sat his mug down on the desk before walking away again. A few moments later, he was wheeling his desk chair out of his office and next to her. "You get logged in?"

Sage nodded, sliding back under the desk fully. "Yes, I checked the emails and there are a few I want to circle back to after you show me how to do the bills."

"Focused on the money, that's why you're the one," he teased.

Sage giggled before leaning over to kiss him, despite trying to remain professional.

Julian groaned as he stepped off the elevator at the scene before him. "Really y'all. At work?"

Startled, the couple jumped a little as Sage let her hand fall from Pierre's chin. "Shut up, Julian. It's your fault I even have to work here."

Julian narrowed his eyes on his soon-to-be cousin. "I didn't tell her to quit."

"Might as well have," Sage mumbled. Julian was about to say something smart, but Pierre jumped in.

"You got something pressing for today?" he asked. "I'm going to show her how to put the invoices in."

"You need me to do anything for you?" she asked. Julian noted the code switch to a more professional tone and decided to follow suit.

"I actually have some SOP's I can send you."

Sage's eyes widened. "That would be great. Thanks."

"I'm not all bark," he said, smirking at her surprised face. Sage rolled her eyes. "That would be great. Thanks," he mocked her. Sage laughed before picking up a pen and throwing it at him.

"You make me sick," she said. Julian smiled at her before walking to his office. Once he sat down, he smiled to see a notification from Tessica. It was an invitation to a family bbq. Instead of responding to her text message, he decided to Facetime her.

"What's up, beautiful."

Tessica smiled. "I didn't call because I knew you were working."

"I just got here," he said.

"That means you have work to do."

Julian sighed. "Stop it. What you doing?"

"Looking over these job offers," she said. Julian smiled. "Trying to decide which one I want."

"Both of them decent," he said, having seen them the night before.

"I know but both have different benefits I kind of want. This remote job looks the best though."

"So what's up with this bbq?"

"Just something light mom is putting together. She thought I was going to leave but now that I'm about to accept a job here, she wants to officially welcome me home."

Julian laughed. "Miss Ann does the most sometimes."

Tessica eyed him, playfully. "Not too much on my mom."

He smiled. "So what? I'm supposed to be your date? You trying to announce us being back together or something."

"If I had something to announce I would. You still playing like you hurt."

"Never been one to play," he said. "You just want me to forgive you on your time. That's not how this works."

Tessica sighed, looking up at the ceiling. Julian knew that meant she wanted to throw a tantrum but was containing herself. "Don't come then, Julian."

He laughed. "You funny."

"It wasn't a joke. I'm not about to keep having this conversation with you. This hot and cold act you got going on is annoying at this point. I never cheated on you. I was a legit girlfriend. You didn't even discuss dropping out with me knowing the plan we made for OUR future. You just decided and expected me to go along with it. Yes, I was wrong for breaking up with you. I've told you that. I miss you. I want to be with you now. If that's not what you want then cool, I tried. But I'm not about to keep kissing your ass while you play the fence. Make a decision and let me know what it is."

Julian laughed, unamused, as Tessica ended the call. He thought about calling back to argue, but knew deep down she was right. The last few weeks, he'd been testing her to see how much she would take. He could admit to being purposely mean, wanting her to react a certain way to see if she was serious about getting back together. He was being childish, but it was only because Julian still had feelings for Nicole. Her snapping and quitting was a reaction that he didn't expect, but he knew things changed when she found out about Tessica.

Instead of dwelling on his complicated love life, Julian pushed himself into work for the rest of the morning. He could hear Pierre and Sage moving around the office. He wasn't in a social mood, so he stayed at his desk for most of the day. Pierre interrupted him around 2 o'clock.

"Sage going to pick up some Sugarfire, text her what you vant." Julian nodded before grabbing his phone. "What's wrong vith you? You been cooped up in here all day."

"Let me ask you something," Julian said. "You think I'm ripping for dealing with Tessica again?"

"Let me ask you something," Pierre said, sitting down in the :hair in front of Julian's desk. "Why do you want to? And you 'eally done with Nicole?"

"It's Tessica," Julian said. Pierre frowned. "I know you hate vhen I say that…but that's what it is."

"And Nicole?"

Julian shrugged, not really sure how to answer.

"You know what I think?" Pierre asked, Julian just looked at ıim. "You knew you weren't that into Nicole."

"I was," Julian said. "I just wasn't THAT into her."

Pierre laughed. "That's what I said. You got bored and she was ıvailable. I told you not to go there."

"Yeah, well I did so sue me."

"I don't know why you still stuck on Tessica, but you knew /ou wanted her as soon as you heard she was divorced, bro. Admit t."

"What you got against Tess?" Julian asked, ignoring Pierre's ıuestion.

"I don't have anything against her. I'm just questioning if she vants you for the right reasons. She left you when you didn't go vith her life plan. What happens now? What if you decide ›omething she doesn't like again? She's just gonna up and leave?"

Julian sighed. "She seems different…"

Pierre threw his hands up in the air. "I'm not trying to talk you ›ut of wanting her. I just want you to be careful. Y'all were cool ogether, but y'all were kids. It might not be the same vibe."

But it was for Julian. Each time he hung out with Tessica, ninus the arguing, he felt the same way he felt all those years ago about her. Julian couldn't recall a time when he didn't vibe wit Tess. Even after she broke up with him, he would see her on socia media and wish he could be near her. Yes, he was pissed off tha she ended their relationship and married the next guy. He wante her to choose him then and the fact that she admitted to makin that mistake was gratifying to Julian. She was wrong. He knew i She knew it. Now it was time to move on.

"I do want her," he admitted.

"Get her then," Pierre said. "Stop holding what happened ove her head before she decides to stop playing the game….And yo owe Nicole an apology."

Julian chuckled. "She not gonna get it. Did way too much."

Pierre shook his head before standing up to leave. "Reckless."

Julian raised an eyebrow at his cousin. "I can recall you no wanting to apologize to Sage either."

"We talking about you right now," Pierre said, laughing. "No me."

Thirteen | No One Else

"Maybe I was too mean," Tessica vented to Naja on Facetime. "I just…he's annoying."

"Um hum," Naja said, smiling. "I can't believe you're staying there."

"You can always come visit, Naj."

"I know…but anyway. Have you talked to him since then?"

"He hasn't called or anything. He did like a post I made," she said, rolling her eyes. "I hate that."

"It is mad weird," Naja said. "You think he'll still come to the bbq?"

Tessica shrugged, fixing her hair in the camera. "I honestly don't know but if he doesn't, I'm done. I can't keep sitting in limbo while he plays with other women."

"Tess, you did just pop up out of nowhere expecting him to commit."

She frowned. "What's wrong with that? I'm not holding a gun to his head, he can say no and leave me alone to do whatever he wants."

Naja laughed. "You are so spoiled."

"It's really his fault though."

"And Brenden's?" Tessica shook her head.

"Naj, honestly…Brenden and I were safe choices for each other. I love him, but I was never in love. I made a mistake of letting fear make me leave Julian. I want to make it up to him. I want to be what I said I would always be for him. He just has to let me."

"He'll come," Naja said, being optimistic. Although Tessica put on a brave face, she had no confidence that he would.

"Party for Me," by Jhene and Ty Dolla Sign was playing in the backyard when Tessica finally made it downstairs. She knew that was her cousin, Cree's, doing. Cree was an event planner and although Tessica didn't want them to make a big deal about her being home, Miss Ann hired her to set up the bbq.

She smiled as Cree caught her coming down the hallway towards the kitchen. "Welcome home for real for real," she said, putting a crown on her head. Tessica laughed.

"Really?"

"Yes, leave it on or I'm telling Auntie."

"You didn't have to do all this," Tessica said, seeing a little of the decorations outside from where she stood.

"Since the pandemic, I haven't done much so this gave me an excuse. It's covid-friendly. All the tables are 6 feet apart and it's only a few chairs at each. Masks, sanitizer, I'm checking temperatures. We're good."

Tessica smiled before looking down at her dress. "This okay?" Tessica was more casual than she usually dressed for a party. Since she was home and it was a bbq, she opted for a two-piece lounge set that she would be comfortable in while still cute.

"You look fine, per usual," Cree said. She moved to stand next to her and put her arm around her shoulder. "Let's go."

Tessica nodded before letting Cree lead her outside. It wasn't a lot of people and Tessica was grateful. Numbers were going up and down with covid and she didn't want to be too risky with her loved ones' lives for the sake of a party.

While moving around, Tessica could feel the love from her family. She was finally excited to be home now that she'd accepted a job offer. It was a remote project engineer position. Her salary would afford her to find a place, but she planned on staying home for a little while. She missed her parents and they were okay with that plan.

Tessica giggled when she heard her mother exclaiming that "her baby was home." She sighed when she saw Julian's parents walk in but he wasn't with them. She sent Naja a text to let her know that he wasn't coming. Naja told her to grab a drink and relax so that's what she did.

A few hours of socializing left her restless and ready to be alone. Everyone seemed to be content with food and their own conversations, so she made her way further into the yard. She smiled as she carefully climbed into the bench swing, swaying under her favorite tree.

Being in that moment allowed her to calm her mind and think about her next steps. It was more than likely Julian wouldn't be part of her homecoming plan, so she had to move accordingly. It wasn't something she was happy about, but she would accept it if she had to.

Tessica tried hard to hide her smile as Julian came through the patio door. She swung her feet as her heart stilled itself. She prayed he would come, but the look on his face told her she wasn't out of the woods just yet. She wanted to jump up and meet him halfway but quickly decided against it. He had to make this walk on his own if he really wanted to be with her.

"I'd be childish to say I'm still mad at something you did years ago," he said, stepping so close in her space that she had to stop swinging to avoid hitting him. "That doesn't mean my trust for you is all here."

Tessica nodded. "I get that...I deserve that."

Julian sighed, running his right hand over his fade and down his face. "I'd really be childish to sit and act like I don't love your entitled...stubborn...sensitive...impatient…"

"I get it, Ju," Tessica said, rolling her eyes. He chuckled before reaching for her hand and pulling her to stand up. Tessica hurried to her feet, eager to be in his personal space. It was one of the places she always felt safe. Tessica would continue kicking herself for letting that go but was hoping he would give her a chance to actually redeem herself.

"It's always been you," he said. Tessica immediately started crying before placing both her hands on his face and kissing him. "Cry baby."

"Shut up," she whined, kissing him again. "You mean that?"

"I do," he said, nodding. "But I need you to understand this isn't back then, Tess. We're not where we were and it's going to take some time."

She nodded. "I get it. I don't care...as long as you're mine."

Julian cleared his throat. Tessica frowned, watching him reach into his back pocket. More tears fell when he held his hand up and opened it enough for the pendant of her necklace to drop and dangle from his finger. It was the diamond moon pendant that she'd given back to him when she broke up with him.

"You...kept it?"

He nodded while frowning, looking at the necklace. "I wanted to throw it away...just could never bring myself to do it."

Tessica's heart broke. She really had no excuse for why she left him the way she did and that made it even more devastating. All the years they missed out on. It was a wonder to her that he would even take her back.

"I love you, Ju," she whispered. Julian sighed before unclasping the necklace and putting it on her. She waited until it was secure to run the pendant between her fingers as she looked up at him.

"I love you, too, Tess." He eyed her. "Don't make me regret it."

"I won't," she said, confidently. "You won't." He nodded before kissing her forehead. Tessica giggled before pulling him to sit down on the swing with her. He put one leg up on the seat and the other dangled. She slid between his legs, sitting sideways and leaning her side against his chest. He kissed her forehead again and she laughed.

"Why you giggling so much?" he whispered in her ear.

Tessica shrugged. "I feel 18 right now," she admitted. Julian laughed before wrapping both of his arms around her shoulders.

"I know right," he confessed. Tessica quickly looked up at him and they both laughed. "Childish."

"So," she said, sticking her tongue out. "Am I okay to assume you're not messing with your secretary anymore? It's me and you right?"

Julian waited until she looked directly at him to nod. Tessica sighed in relief. "She don't work for us anymore either."

"You fired her?" she asked.

Julian shook his head. "But enough about that. I'm hungry and your mom is fixing my plate."

Tessica pouted as he tapped her shoulder to make her sit up. He smiled down at her once he stood up, leaning down to kiss her multiple times until she smiled.

"Don't be spoiled baby," he said, standing up again. Tessica bit her lip from the feeling his attention brought. "You know I came here for you."

Tessica pushed his leg with her foot before he laughed. "Go eat with your smooth self."

"I'll be right back," he said, walking off. Tessica watched her mom's face light up as Julian walked back over to her. She shook her head, content.

"Mine," she thought. *"Just like it's supposed to be."*

Fourteen | Loving You Blind

"So you're just going to get an abortion without telling him?"

Nicole looked up at Raina and frowned. "Don't act like you like him now."

"Liking him and believing he has a right to know he knocked you up are two different things."

"I can't have a baby with someone who doesn't want me," Nicole yelled.

"You can, you just don't want to."

It had been 2 months since she quit her job at Harris Trucking & Construction. Two months since she'd seen Julian Harris. Nicole could finally think of him without wanting to cry. That was until the pregnancy test she took was positive.

Nicole was scared, she had no idea what her next move was and quitting her job was the worst thing she could've done. Now, thanks to that stupid move she couldn't file for unemployment. Not only that, she had lost what she thought was the man of her dreams. Nicole heard this enough from her friends and family but now she was starting to believe that she was just a horrible decision-maker. No one but Raina knew she was pregnant and she wanted to keep it that way.

"I haven't made up my mind all the way," Nicole admitted. "But either way, he won't know about it."

Raina sighed. "I'm going to let you have that for right now."

Nicole rolled her eyes. How her cousin was trying to dictate her life was beyond her, but she would let that comment go. She had other things to deal with.

"I'll call you when I get home."

"Make sure you do."

Nicole hung up the phone before strolling out of the store towards her car. Once she had her groceries loaded, she got inside and snatched her mask off. She skipped through the shuffled playlist on her phone as she drove home. She happened to skip every gospel song that came on because she knew if she listened to it right now that she would really cry. Against her better judgment, she stopped skipping songs when "What's Coming is Better," came on. Finding herself singing the lyrics, Nicole began to cry as her soul cried out for a change.

"God, You're the only one who can get me through this. I have to believe that what's coming is better than where I've been."

What was she going to do with a baby? Nicole had no desire to be a single mother. She wasn't even sold on having kids at all. She always used to say that she would if her husband wanted some, but she would be okay without them. She tried to focus on the road as her and Julian's relationship flashed in her mind. She knew now that she couldn't even call it that. She knew the last time he came over had to be the conception date and it made her sick to her stomach. Nicole honestly didn't even want to have sex that day, but she did it because she thought it would make him stay.

She stalked his social media and it was clear that he and his high school sweetheart were together. He had no shame in posting her. It wasn't long after she quit either. What hurt her feelings was all the things she did for him. Cooking when he wanted. Letting him come over and lay with her whenever he wanted. Being available to him. Making sure her appearance was nice whenever she knew he'd be around. Curving other men as if she were taken. It was evident that Nicole was a good woman, but that didn't mean Julian wanted her.

"Can't catch a bee with honey that doesn't want yours," Nicole mumbled to herself as she wiped her face, parking in her driveway. "Uh!"

Nicole cursed at herself while going inside the house, almost forgetting to get her groceries. She dropped her purse and keys on the counter and before she made it back out of the door, she tripped over a lone shoe in the hallway. Once she fell, instead of getting up, she kicked the shoe out of her way and pushed her back against the wall of her foyer.

"Why is this my life?" she screamed at no one. She sat there for a while, trying to collect her emotions enough to get up and get her food out of the car. By the time she had her groceries put away, Nicole had calmed down.

She contemplated calling Julian to give him the news but because she was unsure of his reaction, she decided against it. If he wanted the baby, she wasn't sure she could co-parent with him. Nicole was honest with herself that if he didn't want the baby, that would break her heart even more.

It was a hard pill to swallow, but Nicole had to take accountability for her role in how everything went down. She had decided to love Julian blindly. She believed his actions instead of his words and that backfired on her. Although her life and her decision about being a mother were up in the air, one thing Nicole knew for sure was that she wouldn't love blindly again.

Ever.

Loving You Blind

Coming Soon

www.ingramcontent.com/pod-product-compliance
Lightning Source LLC
LaVergne TN
LVHW020641100826
845148LV00012B/2287

* 9 7 9 8 9 8 5 2 0 6 0 1 2 *